F rom
Lo
Alg
to small huts,
Harvest goes in search of the beautiful,
missing, Helen Seferis.

Everyone wants Helen—all those who
have read her memoirs that is—for her
book is ripe with recantings of wild sexual
experiences, taboo brushes with lust and
the evolving knowledge that a woman can
be just her senses—a ripe, ready mass of
flesh and nerve endings devoted to pleasure.

Everyone wanted the beautiful, flaxen-
haired nymph—and one man risked his
life to find her. He would be the one to
ultimately claim her for his own.

Also by
ALEXANDER TROCCHI

Young Adam
White Thighs
School for Sin
Helen and Desire
Thongs

THE CARNAL DAYS
of
HELEN SEFERIS

ALEXANDER TROCCHI

MASQUERADE BOOKS, INC.
801 SECOND AVENUE
NEW YORK, N.Y. 10017

First Masquerade Book Edition 1990

First printing December 1990

Second printing March 1993

ISBN 1-878320-086-5

Cover design by Juli Getler

Manufactured in the United States of America
Published by Masquerade Books, Inc.
801 Second Avenue
New York, N.Y. 10017

Chapter 1

"It's Lord Grisskillin. He wants to speak to you."

Laura held the palm of her hand across the mouthpiece of the receiver and fixed me with the amused stare of her green eyes.

Laura is my secretary. Her voice cannot help being confidential, rich, husky, issuing like an improper suggestion from her immaculately made-up lips. She is one of the few women I know whom one can kiss without spreading her mouth around her chin. When her lips draw away they have the same cool sensual perfection as before. You must meet her some time. She'll make you wish you'd never been born.

Imagine a woman of five feet six inches. Her slow green eyes are laconic under smoky long-lashed eyelids. Imagine her with flame-red hair, cut short as an urchin's—a fashion amongst sophisticated women. Imagine a wind-blown appearance at her high cheekbones. Imagine the sleek lines of a mature woman with the clean cut of a racehorse and legs longer and more perplexing than history. You like the smooth set of her hips? The sustained nervousness of her buttocks under her well-tailored skirts? Her breasts rising upwards from a long lean belly tapering to perfection at the waist? Stranger, you are on dangerous ground. Better retreat at once to your semi-detached respectability. She is not for you. Ask your wife. Ask your old mother. Take it from me.

I once had the notion to marry her myself. I confess I went so far as to sleep with her.

We holed up in a hotel and just fucked and fucked and fucked. And I'll never forget what it was like to be buried deeply into the luscious, pink, sweet pussy lips of the green-eyed sex queen with the red, flowing, flaming hair. That hair, it's her real color; I know because I feasted my eyes upon the same red, flaming color in her muff and I tasted those sweet, soft red pussy hairs in my mouth when I went down between the legs of the Laura Goddess and licked so delicately on the soft, petal like folds of her pussy flower.

Ah, it was a glorious moment in time, a time when my cock was a red-hot love poker and it was poking the inner sanctum of my sexy, sharp, snide secretary, who, in that moment in time, was not too proud to spread the long, lean legs apart for her boss so he could probe the depths of her pussy. And it was a tight one. So tight, it sucked me right in, right to the core of her, right to her womb.

If only I'd had a camera to capture the sight of my long, fat, hard prick sliding in and out, in and out, oh yes, in and out between the pink, pink pussy lips and the soft, red pussy hairs; I can still feel the way she sucked me back into her when I pulled out, and the way her cunt muscles closed in around my rod, and the way I could feel her asshole tighten and her legs and hips tense as she pressed herself up, up, up toward my groin. "More cock," her legs, hips and pussy were saying, although she never quite used those words.

She'd wrap her legs around my butt, and pull me down onto her giving me no choice but to fuck, fuck, fuck her in that hotel room. I never wanted to come out, I didn't even want to come because it was so good, I didn't want it to stop.

I'll never forget the first time she made me come; it was in her mouth. She took my prick in her two hands and plunged it between her wonderful lips and sucked on my meat like it was a lollipop and she was a kid trying to get all the flavor out of it.

She licked off the juices gathered from contact with her cunt, she sucked away the creamy cunt emissions, and she went for the thick, ivory liquid of love—and she got it.

It didn't take long, my cock, pressed between her lips, her hands holding my balls, my rod, moving up and down, my cock moving in and out and oooooh, oooooh, explosion... right between those lips. I looked lovingly at Laura, some of my jism dripping down her chin. She swallowed it whole! And she looked at me, dead in the eyes with those big, green peepers of hers. And I never wanted to stop, never wanted to let her have my come that first time, afraid it would be so final, so complete. I wanted more...more of the forbidden fruit of Laura. I could have stayed forever, fucking in that hotel.

A week later, by a fortunate accident, the hotel caught fire and I was rescued by firemen. The light of day hurt my eyes and I had to wear smoked glasses for a fortnight. I don't know what she does with those who don't get away, but if an anxious relative wants information he had better try another agency.

"It sounds urgent," Laura said.

"It's always urgent," I said. "I never met anyone who didn't take himself seriously."

"Are you going to speak to him? He's breathing in my ear."

"Don't be disrespectful," I said. "Lord Grisskillin was a friend of my mother."

"I am not to blame for the coincidence," said Laura sweetly, and, removing her hand from the mouthpiece, she said: "Mr. Harvest will speak to you now."

I walked across the office and took the telephone.

"Hello?"

The voice came back to me from the other end of the telephone: "Hello, is that you Anthony, my boy?"

"Yes sir." The jade green eyes at the other side of the desk narrowed in amusement.

"I'm so glad I got hold of you, my boy. Look, I want you out at my place tonight, about eight if you can manage it. It's important."

"It's important," Laura said helpfully.

I gave her what was intended to be a withering look.

"Can you come?"

"Well, it's rather short notice, you know, sir."

"Yes, I'm sorry about that, Anthony. I wouldn't ask you unless it really were important."

"All right. Eight o'clock, you said?"

"Not any later."

"I shall do my best."

"Thank you, my boy." The receiver clicked at the other end.

"You had an appointment with Mr. Busby at eight," said Laura as I replaced the instrument.

"Must you always listen to my conversations?"

"Your friends have such loud voices."

"You're very impertinent."

"You've said so before."

"I'm saying it again."

"You're like a grooved gramophone record," she said. "I don't know why I work for you. Do you know, I once thought you were interesting!"

"You would still if I had agreed to marry you."

"Mr. Harvest, I wouldn't marry you if you were the last man on earth. I would rather tame an ape."

"I don't for a moment suppose that you would experience any difficulty," I said, returning to my desk.

"And what about Mr. Busby?"

"That's what I pay you for, to make excuses."

But, like the efficient secretary she was, she was already on the telephone and her honey sweet voice would have neutralized the acids in the stomach of any dyspeptic.

An hour later, at five thirty p.m., I left the office.

"Want to come with me to Grisskillin's? His cook is one of the best in the country."

"No, thank you," she replied. "I have a date."

"Unlucky fellow," I said. "Nothing can save him but an Act of God."

Laura smiled.

"All God's acts are pre-established," she said with satisfaction, "and you forget, Mr. Harvest, that I am one of them."

Lord Grisskillin's estate was an hour's drive from town, not far from Great Missenden in Buckinghamshire. At a few miles distance was Chequers, the country home of British Prime Ministers. These came and went, frequently guests at his famous dinner table, but old Grisskillin, the wry old Scots financier, lingered on.

A word about the man. He never married, but was reputed to have an insatiable curiosity about married women. Had he lived a hundred years before, I am afraid he would have long ago perished in a duel, for his generosity to married women was so extensive as to be almost compromising. Opinion was divided as to his motives. Some said that he had such a deep respect for the institution of marriage that he used his great fortune to reward the virtuous wives of his friends. Others, more cynical, were of the opinion that he was so afraid of being tricked into marriage that he "rented" the wives of other men, paying so liberally for that favor, as to make any problems with the husbands highly improbable. Ah, and there were the mumblings that Grisskillin simply liked to fuck with women already betrothed. He could have the experience of loving a beautiful married woman, without the bother of marriage. The married ladies, I'm sure one might assume, were already "broken in," experienced and honorable sluts. I would not vouch any of these opinions. By a strange twist of fate I am barred from exercising my detecting talents in this direction. Were I to do so, I should, to put it bluntly, run the risk of establishing my own illegitimacy. When Grisskillin, his hand on my shoulder, says "my boy," any desire I have to look into the past life of this old gentleman is immediately and effectively aborted. As far as I am concerned, his notorious generosity to the wives of other men will remain a dark and comfortable enigma.

I changed my clothes at my bachelor flat off Mayfair and was soon seated in my sleek black Mercedes, outstripping the other traffic on the road to Great Missenden. This car, far too big and far too fast for British roads under normal conditions, is amongst my few self indulgences. The others I could list under the general heading: pleasures of the intellect and of the senses. When I am alone, I give myself over to the pleasures of the intellect. I would rather read or think than talk. Conversation seems to me to be without exception a practical act, a game of adjustment within another's categories, rather than an intellectual exercise. When I am not alone, I prefer the company of females for the simple reason that they have an intuitive understanding of the fact that what is said is of little or no significance except as a means of shortening that awful distance between the drawing room and the bedroom. In the latter I give myself over, body and soul, to the pleasures of the senses. Just like I enjoy a challenging case, I enjoy a challenging female, one who not so much puts up a fight, as she demands a certain quality from a man—because I love to fulfill any order for quality fucking and loving.

I love, for example, to go down on a woman and virtually torture her with the pleasures of my tongue on her cunt, to tickle her quim with a feather light tongue lashing or a flickering clit licking. They squirm, they wiggle, they shake their hips and they press their pussies into my face. And they spend their creamy emissions into my mouth.

This makes me extremely, extraordinarily hot, and hard, and ready to come myself. But first, I even like to torture them with pleasure, just a bit more, and press my lips onto the tender, raw bud of a clitoris that's just come and bring it back to life. Oh, this drives most women crazy with pleasure.

"It's too much," they say. "I can't take it," they whine. But I press on, still, and pull the delicate clitoris petal into my mouth, and suck it between my rolling tongue, and lightly, ever-so-lightly, gnaw on it, until I feel it rise once again in my mouth.

They resist. They squeeze closed their cunt lips, they press together their thighs, because it feels too good—too good. But I adore giving the greatest, profoundest of pleasures to the lovely, sexy, sensuous and desirable sex—the female gender.

For the rest of the time, I am a hard working detective with an insatiable curiosity about the motives which lead human beings to murder, theft, rape or adultery. You could say that each of my endeavors requires and relates to a good deal of passion.

In slightly over an hour, 7:48 P.M. on the dial of my car clock, I ran the Mercedes, into the drive of Henry Park and drew up on the crisp white gravel outside the main door.

Lord Grisskillin himself greeted me in the hall.

"Anthony, my boy, I'm so glad you could come! Give Parkins your things and step into the library with me. I want to talk to you before the others come."

After passing my coat and hat to the butler, I followed my host into a room that smelled of leather and cigar smoke. In this room, it occurred to me, the commercial policies of half the world received a direction. Three walls were almost entirely lined by leather-backed books, from Plato to Klausewitz, from Aristotle to Marx. Two paintings by the reigning president of the Royal Academy were in undue prominence on the third wall. That was one thing my host and I had never seen eye to eye about. I deplored his taste in pictures. He talked vaguely of safe investments. When I pointed out that works by R.A. presidents seldom retained value for long after the death of their perpetrators, he murmured, probably with reference to his lack of knowledge regarding art, something about the danger of buying a pig in a poke. My exhortations were quite useless.

12

Considering his vast experience, he could not see why I should know more about art than he. I was bright and clever, but hardly "sound"; that is to say, I could not put my signature to a five-figure cheque. How to trust me then in anything which involved making an investment?

"Sit down, sit down. Whiskey and soda?"

I nodded. He poured from the decanter and passed me the soda syphon. Then he ensconced himself in the leather chair behind his desk. He was a type of fine old Scotsman who is still lean in his late sixties, with penetrating grey eyes under shaggy grey eyebrows and a head of silver hair which he would never lose. He poured ordinary water into his own whiskey from a jug on the desk.

"I wanted you, Anthony, because, do you see, you can't have a Yard man without all the world knowing about it. Have you ever seen a policeman trying to be discreet?"

I tried to look sympathetic. For myself, having worked with Scotland Yard while I was in Intelligence during the war, I have an expert's admiration for their intelligence and discretion. Grisskillin, however, whose experience in these matters was limited to that which he derived from our popular detective story writers, could not be expected to see things in that light. For him, a policeman had big feet and no table manners.

"What's the trouble?" I asked.

"No trouble exactly," he said quickly. "I'm giving a reception here tonight for the daughter of a friend of mine. I just wanted to have a good man on hand to see that there's no trouble."

"Why should there be any trouble?"

Grisskillin looked at me as though I were something which had crawled out from under a stone.

13

I flushed. "I mean why tonight rather than any other night?"

"I've just told you. There's the daughter of a friend of mine coming."

I tried to be patient.

"Who is she?"

"Her name's Nadya Pamandari. She's the daughter of Pamandari of Bombay."

"You don't say!" I said, simulating intelligent surprise, although, to tell the truth, I had heard neither of Miss Pamandari nor of her father.

"Ah! Now you see the point!" said my host with evident satisfaction. "I thought for a moment, I'd been mistaken in you. As you can see for yourself, it's not every evening I am responsible for the only child of Pamandari."

"Quite so," I said. I took a shot in the dark. "She'll be wearing jewelry?"

"Probably nothing but," said Grisskillin wryly. "But that's only half the story. She's flying in from Paris tonight and while she's in England I shall be responsible for her. Well, the trouble is, she absolutely refuses to stay here. She's taken a suite at Cedal's. If anything happened to her, her father would hold me responsible."

"I don't see how he could do that," I said.

"There are some things, my dear boy, that I despair of your ever seeing," Grisskillin said testily. "But fortunately, in this instance, it doesn't matter whether you see or not. I am telling you. Pamandari would hold me responsible. For this reason, I am going to make quite sure that nothing happens to the child. Do you understand?"

"Quite."

"In that case, we can go on. I haven't seen this girl for ten years, but from all reports she looks like Sheba and has the morals of a tomcat."

I brightened considerably at this.

"You don't say!" I said.

"If you make one more fatuous remark like that, I'll show you the door and call in the Yard," said my host.

"Of course, you are at liberty to do that at any time," I said pleasantly, "But if my memory serves me correctly you seemed a short while ago to be unwilling to do so." I reached over his desk and poured myself another shot of whiskey.

"I see your manners haven't improved since you were here last," Grisskillin said with a grunt.

"My manners, like Miss Pamandari's morals have lost their original brightness," I admitted with a smile.

"That'll be enough of that," said Grisskillin with a twinkle in his eye. "Whatever she is or does is not our concern. But she must leave these shores as she came to them, in one piece."

"That much I understand," I said. "Now, you say she has been in Paris. Who looks after her while she's there?"

"Ah, I see we're getting down to business at last. You'd better make some notes." He paused, waiting, I suppose, for me to produce a notebook. When I sat without moving, he said: "Are you not going to make a note of this?"

"I'm all ears," I said pleasantly.

"Of course it's not for me to criticize your methods of work," he began.

"Of course not," I said.

"Very well. Nadya Pamandari must be eighteen or nineteen years of age, good-looking, with a perfectly splendid figure."

"And with the morals of a tomcat."

Grisskillin affected to ignore me. "She came to

15

Europe in the company of another woman whose name is, I believe, Helen Seferis. This person disappeared at Marseilles. I don't think she need concern us. From Marseilles she went north to Paris in the company of an Italian duke, a man called Mario Ratsonli. I believe she is bringing him tonight. As far as I can make out, his morals are no better than hers. He is without visible means of support, but has been seen cashing checks at a Bombay bank. They are signed by Miss Seferis."

"You have been busy! It's getting to be quite a tangle, isn't it?"

"If you wish me to recapitulate in order for you to take notes in a systematic way, I shall," he said drily.

"Thanks, but it won't be necessary," I said.

"Just as you wish," he said.

"One point before you go on," I said. "Have you by any chance written to Mr. Pamandari for information?"

"Don't be a fool! Do you expect me to tell him that his daughter's a whore?"

"I doubt if she takes money, sir!"

"Eh, what do you mean?"

"I mean that I shouldn't call her a whore if she didn't."

"Pah! She's immoral, immodest, that's what I mean."

"I shouldn't be at all surprised if her father were already aware of this. After all, he's had more time to observe her than you, if you will excuse my saying so."

"Maybe so, but it's not for me to remind him. I shall proceed. She has been in Paris for over six months. So has this cohort of hers. I had to instruct my Paris agent to burn the file and to proceed no further with investigations. It is not a pretty story. And now she has taken it into her head to carry her dissipation to England."

16

"It sounds all very interesting."

"I suspected you would think so. However, that is not my concern. She must leave England with, if not her virginity, at least her person and property intact."

"And her ducal escort?"

"I'm not concerned with him. The world would probably be a better place if he broke his disgusting neck!"

"You realize that my time is expensive?"

"I suspected it, although I see no reason why it should be."

"It will cost you a thousand pounds a month."

"The Devil it will! I'll give you twenty pounds a week."

"In that case," I said, standing up, "I must be off. I have another appointment."

"Sit down, young man, and don't be impertinent! Why should I pay you all that money? It's highway robbery!"

"Call it what you please." I said pleasantly, "but that is my fee."

"For looking after a girl?"

"A girl with the morals of a tomcat."

"I don't see what her morals have got to do with it!"

"It is a 24-hour-a-day job, I should suppose," I said calmly. "If you pay me a thousand pounds a month you are in fact grossly underpaying me. I am, of course, gambling on the possibility that sometimes she likes to sleep. If she sleeps eight hours a day, which I doubt, you will be paying me just over £2 an hour which is considerably less than you pay your dentist."

Grisskillin grunted, contracting his brows in the familiar lines of calculation.

"It is also," I continued, "considerably less than

17

my usual hourly fee. If the price still seems to you too high, however, I shall be glad to send you one of my watchdogs at half that price."

The old financier waved the suggestion aside.

"I want none of your Boy Scouts in this business," he said, "but I warn you, Anthony, if anything happens to this girl while she is in England, I'll sue you for every halfpenny you've got!"

"I don't guarantee anything," I said. "I am not an insurance company. I am a private investigator. And now, if you still want to engage me, I should like the first month's salary in advance."

"Now!"

"You can write a check," I said helpfully.

The though hadn't struck him, but now, realizing at last that I was quite serious, he reached into the drawer in front of him and with no further comment made out a check for the required amount.

As I folded it neatly and placed it in my wallet, he said:

"I have it on good authority that you are a reliable man."

It was almost a question. I smiled without replying.

"I can hardly believe it," he said.

"I don't see why not."

"Anyway," he said, getting up, "I dislike the breed."

I coughed discreetly. I had no desire to stir up the embers of a past so mercifully obscure.

Alone in the library, I heard the first cars arriving. I poured myself another whiskey, found myself regretting the absence of my dear, wry, secretary, Laura—I could never quite get over Laura—and planted myself in one of the comfortable leather armchairs,

and slipped into the memory of a fantasy come true.
I looked almost sentimentally across space and into
a hotel room at the far end of which, Laura's head
tilted slightly backwards as she drew the blouse off
the superb curvature of her shoulders. Laura, for the
first time and with the haughty movements of a
sophisticated woman, undressed for me. We had
decided to sleep together almost casually, or so anyway it appeared on the surface. But, at the same
time, I remember that when there was nothing left to
say—dinner was over and we had stubbed the fourth
or the fifth cigarette—nothing left to do except to
put in words the naked terms of the compact whose
urgency had grown and expressed itself in a sudden
meeting of eyes as course following course in the
exclusive little restaurant where we were eating; her
lips remained slightly apart and her breath, laced, I
felt, with the warm corrosive moisture of sex,
seemed to come from between teeth clenched slightly in anticipation; and I remember my own breath,
trammelled, the needling emission of sweat at my
chest and on the tense surfaces of my abdomen, as I
fought to break down the paralysis at my throat
which seemed incapable of making the appropriate
verbal gesture just as it was incapable of uttering any
further inanities. Yes, everything was clear to me
then with the clarity born of a sixth sense, with all
the myriad impressions I had of her, the scarlet
gleam of her lower lip, the fragrant, tulip-like texture of her temples and eyelids, the long shadowy
line of her throat hollowing at its base and expanding downward along the smooth and full white slats
of flesh which, immaculately tense from neck to
armpits, sustained the superb poise of the breasts
under her off-the-shoulder blouse, and her eyes
especially, slanting green pools that were somehow

enigmatic and eager at the same time—everything clear, the necessity of saying what I eventually did say, that—for I cannot recall the exact words which would probably sound hollow anyway out of relation to the overpowering physical reality of the moment—I had been talking to one purpose and to one purpose only, at least for the last hour, watching, as I spoke, her eyes, and then the movement of her lips as her husky voice sealed the compact with the admission that she accepted and had all along participated in it. And then, for the first time in a hotel room together, what exultation I experienced as the blouse slipped farther from her shoulders, revealing first the delicate mauve hollows of her armpits and after that, with breath-taking suddenness, the elastic resilience of her full, naked breasts! She shared in my exaltation, naked now from her waist up, her firm tits like small damsons, and a frail trickle of perspiration where her stomach hollowed towards the navel.

I had cupped her breasts in my hands, and pulled her toward me with a gentle tug on her velvet smooth titties. The nipples stood erect, bright pink buds of womanhood beckoning to me from their throne upon her breast, so I kissed them...ever so gently I kissed them with a warm, wet and soothing tongue. Then, pulling her even closer, tugging on them just a bit harder, I sucked on the hardened buds, and nibbled playfully. She moaned, and the sound seemed to echo through her very being and fill the room. I could hear her pleasure, could feel it welling up inside her. And I wanted nothing more than to please her and show her what a man I could be.

I let my hands wander now, down her back, caressing the small of it, and over her buttocks, feeling the soft, velvet skin as my hands pressed against the bottom globes from beneath her skirt and met one another at the crack of her ass.

I spread it open, still sucking on her tits, and pressed a finger between the globes, toward the pink crinkled orifice. Bringing one middle finger to my mouth, I wet it, and placed it back to her ass, lubricating the outer puckered ring so I might venture further.

Her mouth came down on mine now, knocking her titties from their place between my teeth, and she was kissing me with the kind of sweet passion I always suspected was inside her, but had never known intimately before.

Her hands traveled down to her skirt; she undid it. It slid over her trim hips, onto the floor. She stepped out of it and her bottom was entirely free—save for the pink lace garter belt and white silk stockings.

I ran both hands around her hips, her ass, her back and touched her all over until there was not a place on her gorgeous Goddess form that I hadn't laid my hands. Fascinated, I went back to the crack of her ass, reaching it from around her waist, and gently splayed the cheeks apart, poked my finger to the rim of the opening and press against it.

My cock, by then, was a steel rod of pure lust that wanted nothing more than to be buried somewhere in that lovely body.

She reached down, as if reading my thoughts, and released my cock from my trousers. I was engorged to the utmost, and she easily took the huge swollen organ in her hands, kissed the purple head and placed those lips—ah, those lips—over it and took the entire prick into her mouth.

I was afloat in pleasure, a deep thrilling kind of feeling that swept right through my balls, traveled the length of my cock and even sent a twitch of excitement through my asshole.

She started to suck, furiously and fast and with meaning, and I could see the flaming red hair—splayed across her shoulder, arms and now, across my own skin as she moved up and down—and all I wanted to do was run my fingers through it. I did, placing my hands, both of them, atop her head and running them wildly, madly through the gorgeous mop.

Suddenly, seized by the desire to have her, to taste her, to take her, I lifted her by a tug of that gorgeous red mane and tossed her on the bed, and watched her naked body settle atop the sheets. I quickly removed my trousers, my shirt, and got on top of her, my cock poised at the entrance of her cunt.

She opened for me; wide and willing, she spread those legs apart, as those jade green eyes peered into mine, begging that I plug her with my manhood.

I pressed it just at the opening, and pushed in ever-so-slightly. She pushed forward, on it. She wanted more.

I gave her just a taste, just a bit, just a tease and a titillation and then, I whispered: "First, I will pleasure you with my tongue and will thrill you with great feelings of excitement." She shivered, and reacted by pressing her cunt toward my prick, trying to maneuver it in. I knew my refusal would make her cunt even steamier, hungrier.

I got down between those long beautiful legs, and I spread the soft, sweet cunt petals apart and leisurely poked my tongue into the sweet gash between her thighs. It smelled of nature's sweetest woman-scent and the soft odor filled my nostrils. I licked her clit bud, pressing my tongue against the hardened pleasure spot. She wriggled with joy, and tried to escape the intense feeling. I held her hips firmly and began to suck.

"Ooooh, you're driving me crazy," she cooed, that wild mane of red hair flipping back and forth as she tossed her head this way and that. "My cun-t-t is on f-f-fire. Oh please, please, pleeease fuck me. Ooooh, f-fuck me."

I was tempted to jump on top of her and plunge right into that juicy cunt; I had to refrain from doing so. For first, before I put myself deep into the recess of love between her legs, I wanted a taste of that perfect asshole. I used to think she had a bug up her ass. Now I wanted to lick it and suck it right out.

I took one last, long, tantalizing suck on the engorged clit and skillfully flipped her over to her stomach. She was shocked, and her knees were weak from pleasure, but she did as she was told.

"Get on your knees," I commanded playfully, "and stick your butt up in the air."

She did and whimpered: "Will you fuck me from behind? Will you give it to me from that vantage point."

"I've got something more pressing right now," I said, and with that I bent my face over those lovely, round, firm bottomcheeks and began to kiss her ass...all over...little kisses and caresses. I kissed my way to the lovely crack between the globes and began to lick it, up and down, and up and down, until it was quite lubricated with the warm wetness of my mouth. Then, I carefully, artfully pried apart the flesh to reveal the lovely, pink, puckered bung, my fingers pressing it wide apart right at the gates of the opening, I slipped my tongue through the opening and felt it pass through the rim. She tightened for a moment, her sphincter muscle closing in around my tongue. I pressed in further. She moaned.

All I wanted in that moment was to fill her ass with lustful pleasures, to give her great fullness and fulfillment from that prone position. And she wanted it, I could tell, because she began pressing her ass into my tongue, so that in a short time my tongue was buried in her to the hilt and she was moaning like a wild woman.

Her cunt now was a fiery fuck inferno and it begged and pleaded to get filled with a full, satisfying feeling—the kind of feeling that, at that stage, only a big, huge, swollen cock could appease.

Before I gave her my hot rod of pleasure, I made sure that she was totally filled up the ass with my tongue, and now, fingers, which in spreading open the rim were now placed more deeply into the cleft. This drove her quite insane with wanton lust and she almost begged me to fuck her asshole just so she could get it, just so she could get her fill.

But I wanted her cunt and was ready to take it because dear Laura, the Goddess of sophisticated woman, was now a whimpering, pleading, wanton mound of cunt and ass that was at the mercy of my ability to provide fulfillment and release.

"Up on all fours," I commanded, as she'd slumped forward somewhat. "I'm going to fuck you now and give you everything you need. Which hole do you want it in, Laura, which part should I fill first?"

She pressed her ass forward and moaned. I could tell, she was torn between wanting it in both places. I reached my hand down to the floor, where I'd left a little sex toy, wrapped up in a soft, silken bag. It was a small dildo, with a rounded edge and a somewhat

pointy tip. It was meant for moments like this—
when a woman wanted it in her cunt, and her ass.

Her ass was so wet from my lavish tongue fuck
and tongue bath that the dildo slid in easily, gently
and filled her to the brim with a wonderful, full feeling. And next, it was her cunt that would be brim-
ming with that fullness—the fullness of my male
machine.

I slipped it in from behind and it went all the way
in on the first thrust. She groaned, she whimpered
and she pleaded that I press it in even further, against
her womb. I obliged and felt as if my cock was being
pulled in by a warm, firm hand gloved in velvet; it
sucked me forward, it took me to the deepest depths
of pussyland. I was fucking the most amazing cunt on
the planet, filling the holes of a gorgeous, sophisticated redhead whose hair flamed across the pillow as I
flamed across her boldly, plugging her with my huge,
engorged cock.

I reached around to feel for her clit and felt the
bud stiffen between two fingers. As I fucked her,
thrusting my cock in to the balls, while her ass stayed
filled with the dildo, I squeezed the little bud
between a thumb and index finger and felt her cring-
ing, writhing, going crazy beneath the weight of all
this pleasure.

"Everything is beginning to come," she groaned in
that rich, husky voice of hers. "I'm one big, huge,
mound of cunt and come."

She was panting like an animal and pressing ass
against cock, pussy against balls, and clit against fingers as her body began to shake and gyrate in the
most wildly exquisite manner, and I could feel the
cunt muscles twitch and tug at my prick.

And that got me going, the feel of her wet, juice
explosion, and the feel of her tugging me, pulling

me off with her, and suddenly I felt it begin to release and erupt and squirt all over the insides of that silky red haired cunt as I pressed once, then twice, then three, then four more times in her as the last drops of jism exploded in her, and hers dripped out on me.

We fell, her first, then me on top of her, onto the bed in a heap of flesh and rolled over on our sides. The dildo slipped out of her ass, and I caught it, holding the warm, slimy thing in my hand as I closed my eyes serenely. She rested her red-top upon my biceps and took a deep, sultry drag of air. And that was the first time I did it with Laura.

Strangely, as I sat there in Grisskillin's library, I wished to proceed no further with the reverie. I wished to distill from the past only that first proud moment when the fresh white blouse was lowered, when the taut and peerless skin of her upper torso seemed to rise upwards into my sight like the turning belly of a gray shark.

What had I done? What strange uncompromising passion had I inspired in this proud woman? Love? I know that at that moment I was in love. A door closed on the past. The soft tensions at the meeting of our thighs was like curtains idling in the wind.

When Grisskillin spoke from the library door, I swallowed the whiskey at a gulp.

"I trust you are comfortable," he said sarcastically.

"I was thinking," I replied, standing up.

"Since the Germans discovered Hamlet, that has been the curse of western civilization," my host said. "Young men think too much these days, and seldom to the point."

"The sins of the fathers," I said lightly, crossing the room towards him. "It was our unthinking fathers who made the problem."

"Well, if you're ready, I shall introduce you to Miss Pamandari."

"I can think of nothing which would give me more pleasure," I replied bowing my head as I followed him from the room.

Chapter 2

"Nadya, my dear," said Grisskillin to a superb looking, young, olive-skinned woman wearing a low-cut white dress, "I should like to present a young friend of mine, Mr. Anthony Harvest."

The wonderful creature turned smoothly to greet us and her dark eyes considered me from behind the almost insect-like fragility of her soft, fan-shaped eyelashes. The eyes themselves were almond-shaped which gave her whole face an Oriental aspect.

"I am happy to make your acquaintance, Mr. Harvest," she said with a brilliant smile.

I inclined my head without speaking, allowing my eyes to take in the roundly poised tensions under the white silk. An ornate necklace of diamonds set off the fair smooth skin of her throat. I inspected it discreetly before I raised my eyes to meet her dazzling glance. She seemed to glow with the aura of sex.

Grisskillin had already moved off and was in conversation with a Mrs. Buxton-Shoreman, a handsome woman of about fifty, and the wife of a parliamentary Under-Secretary who was known to be on the verge of bankruptcy. As she spoke, the woman's full bosom seemed to tremble sympathetically, and, had I been open to suspicions at that moment—for Grisskillin's head was lowered as he listened to her, so that his eyes, deep-set behind shaggy eyebrows, and the appearance of being riveted on the trembling twin peaks—I should have staked my last sixpence that later, perhaps in a few day's time, discreetly, the financier would take those trembling titties in his hand for a sumptuously pleasing caress. He might even run a tongue around the crinkly nipple buds, and draw them into his warm wet mouth by sucking, ever-so-gently, as the woman began to squirm beneath him, a wetness dripping from between her somewhat wrinkled yet trim, thighs. She seemed, in the moment, to want Grisskillin's silver-haired head buried in her cunt. You could tell!

"You have known Lord Grisskillin for a long time?" Miss Pamandari queried.

"He could almost be said to have brought me up," I replied.

"Ah, you know him well, then! Is that woman his mistress?"

"My dear Miss Pamandari! I know nothing of his personal life!"

"But surely you have eyes, Mr. Harvest. That woman is not too old for love. She is trying to seduce him."

I repressed a smile.

"Your are interested in love, then," I said.

"You have a strange way of speaking, Mr. Harvest."

"How so?"

"I mean one isn't 'interested' in love. One is interested in the arts, one is interested in polo, or cricket, or race horses. But love, no, that is something else."

"I see."

"I sincerely hope you do. Will you dance with me, Mr. Harvest?"

"With the greatest of pleasure!"

I conducted her to the floor where a number of couples were already dancing. She moved into my arms softly, with a swish of her fashionable evening dress, and the warmth of her full thighs seemed to hang, tenuously, against mine as we glided to the center of the floor.

She held herself close against me, her breasts crushed against my chest. Our groins mashed together. Against my will, I felt myself harden. I was slightly embarrassed by this, as it was certainly not my intention to stiffen so against a client, so to speak. Yet it was as if I were a schoolboy again. And she seemed not to mind. In fact, she seemed somewhat delighted by my response, and exerted even more pressure against me. This inspired a heated sex fantasy to play in my brain, a fantasy where the woman with the morals of a tomcat also had the tongue of a tigress, and she hungrily, greedily swished that tongue around my bare organ, making it harder yet. She took my engorged manhood in hand, cupped my swollen balls, and came down on my cock with all of her mouth, taking me into the deep, wet, wild, cocksucking orifice.

The thought of this made me harder still, and it was as if I could not halt my thoughts. I allowed the fantasy to continue as we danced.

I imagined us gloriously entwined in a 69 position—cunt to mouth, cock to mouth, eating each other like hungry animals filled with lust and desire.

Yes, I could just see the dark, almost purple cunt folds; like dusky, sensual petals that would blossom in my mouth. The sweet dewy aroma would waft from between those olive legs and into my flared nostrils and I could breath in the musk of her, the dew of her, the sweet scent of sexed-up cunt.

I'd lick her so softly, so tantalizingly, so joyously, working a tongue from the base of the cunthole and up to the engorged clit. And then, when she was good and hot, I'd come down on the hot, swollen clit like a starved man at dinnertime, and devour it with wildly sexy sucking, licking, and even biting, until I brought her to the very brink of abandonment and erupting desire, just about to come, feeling herself about to release the honey of jism onto my tongue.

She'd press herself, firmly, up to my lips; pushing her cunt even deeper to my mouth. And that's when I'd stick a finger into the wet, juice-filled cunthole and plow into her mushy insides with a finger fucking in and out, in and out, as I suck, suck, suck the juice from her clit.

Meanwhile she was sucking on my cock like a wild woman in heat, trying to take it all deeply into the back of her throat, as far as she could. She played with my balls, fondled them, and jerked my dick up and down, until I, too, was wild with desire to release myself, to explode all over her.

As my come shot out in white spurts all over her mouth and hand, her own juice seeped from her slit into my mouth. And we lapped the juices of sexual joy, she, licking the length of my pole and sucking the white pearls of come from the tip, and me, licking my way deep into her cunthole to catch the salty flavor of her girl-juice. Ah, what a fantasy!

As I held her in my arms, her body still pressed

against my hard-on during the dance, I could feel myself close to coming just by dancing with the olive-skinned nymph, my charge during her stay in London.

Slowly, we finished our dance, our faces calm and cordial, while our bodies cried out to touch, to lick and taste, and the animal in us each imagined what it would be like to be freed from the two layers of clothing that came between us and let loose upon one another.

"You came alone, Miss Pamandari?"

"No. Mario is with me. Mario Ratsonli. He's talking to that blonde over there. He pretends to be in love with me, but he isn't. Since Helen, he won't look at a woman unless she's a blonde."

"How tasteless of him!" I said gallantly.

"Ah, you haven't met Helen!"

"You mean Helen Seferis?"

"How did you know?"

"That would be a long story, Miss Pamandari."

"One which, at another time, in another place, I might find time to listen to," she said softly.

"My time is yours," I said, amused at the truth of my statement.

"I shall not forget," she said, and her eyes, a few inches from my own, were suddenly veiled by the long curve of her eyelashes.

After the dance, she was whisked away from me by one of the many young men present. Her escort, I noticed, was still in conversation with the thin blonde over by the French windows.

I went in search of Parkins, the butler, to have his opinion on the guests. I had been talking to him for about ten minutes, off and on, because he had to constantly be greeting late arrivals, when a footman came in search of me.

"Lord Grisskillin would like to see you, sir, in the library." I nodded, told Parkins to inform me if any character of a suspicious nature was admitted, and made my way to the library to see my host.

He was standing with his back to the fireplace, his brow like thunder.

"Ah, there you are at last!" he said angrily. "A fine mess you've made of things!"

"I don't know what you mean, sir."

"Where the Hell have you been anyway! First you were daydreaming in here and then you disappear altogether and meanwhile Miss Pamandari loses her diamond necklace!"

"Miss Pamandari has lost her necklace," I said in a tone of disbelief. "When did this happen?"

"What a damn fool I was to trust you!" he smoldered. "Someone could have kidnapped her without your noticing it!"

"Look here, Grisskillin," I said, riled at last, "I've taken all I'm going to from you. If it weren't for the fact that you were a friend"—I emphasized the word 'friend'—"of my mother, I should have told you what a pompous old fool you were before now!"

He was staring at me unbelievingly but I continued before he could interrupt me.

"Now you are going to do just as you're told, do you understand?"

At that moment, the door opened, and Nadya Pamandari, a distressed look on her beautiful face, came in.

"If it was only a question of its value," she said at once, "it wouldn't matter, because of course it's insured. But it was a present from my father on my sixteenth birthday."

"Thank God it was insured," Grisskillin said stupidly.

"Please sit down, Miss Pamandari," I said. "And you, Grisskillin, please send a footman to fetch Signor Ratsonli."

"Mario left a few moments ago," Nadya said. "With that blonde, you know. I saw no reason why we should spoil his evening."

Grisskillin turned purple but I held up a hand to silence him.

"I'm afraid, Miss Pamandari, that he took your necklace with him."

Her eyes widened with dislike. "How dare you suggest that Mario would steal from me!"

"Have you any evidence to substantiate your accusation?" Grisskillin said warily.

"Miss Pamandari," I said, "I have no wish to interfere with your private affairs. But if you will take my advice you will not report the loss to the insurance company."

"What are you trying to say?" she said angrily.

"Pah!" Lord Grisskillin exclaimed, "I've wasted enough time with you, Harvest; I'm going to call Scotland Yard."

"Put down that telephone!" I said in a quiet voice, "Get it through your thick skull that nothing was stolen here tonight."

His hand froze on the receiver. Nadya was staring at me wide-eyed.

"The stones that Miss Pamandari wore tonight were fakes," I continued.

"Are you sure of that?"

It was Grisskillin who spoke.

I ignored him. I poured myself a whiskey from the decanter. When I had added soda to my liking and tasted the mixture, I spoke again. "The diamonds were probably removed some time ago," I said. "It could only have been someone who was free to come and go in your bedroom, someone who could borrow them for long enough, or often enough, to have them copied. A maid, therefore, or your friend, Mario; and I should think that he alone had the opportunity to take them from you tonight."

"But it might have been a professional!"

"My dear Miss Pamandari, a professional doesn't steal fake diamonds. I could only have been someone who wanted to cover up a past theft. What was taken tonight was worthless except as evidence that the real stones had, in fact, been removed earlier."

"We had better call the police," Grisskillin said quietly.

"No!" Her retort was like a pistol shot. She sat down. I poured a brandy for her. She accepted it gratefully.

"Perhaps he needed money," I suggested. "After all, Helen Seferis has disappeared. He was no longer getting money from her."

Once again her lovely dark eyes registered amazement.

"How on earth did you know that!"

"We'll discuss it on the way home," I said quietly. "Meanwhile, I'll get your wrap."

We drove in silence along the London road. The lights of the Mercedes picked out trees and hedges like shadows of a strange unnatural world. We were both smoking. Occasionally her hand, with its long slender fingers—the perfectly cultured nails varnished a deep vermilion—moved under the green light of the dashboard to flick the ash from her smoldering cigarette. We had exchanged few words since we rolled off the gravel of the drive onto the main road.

"Unhappy?" I said finally.

"Not exactly," she replied. "Of course it means that I can't see Mario again."

"It all depends on the way you feel about it," I said, watching the rising strip of road ahead. "I mean you were living with him. You didn't grudge him his mistresses, but a man can't have mistresses without money. It's quite understandable that he should have stolen the necklace."

"You think so?"

"Be reasonable," I said. "What would you have done in his place? He tried to arrange the theft nicely, that's to say, so that you wouldn't have to feel bad about him."

"I think you're very immoral." She was smiling.

"Neither moral nor immoral," I replied. "You're not being honest with yourself. You were tired of him anyway. This episode gives you the excuse you were looking for. You wanted to break with him before tonight."

"Why should I be sad then?"

"Histrionics," I said. "You're acting a part. You're a self-indulgent woman."

"You're not very flattering, Mr. Harvest!"

"A flatterer has a short rope," I said, glancing sideways at her. She was still smiling, her lips full, curved and dark in profile. "Anyway," I continued, "I am flattering you. I'm allowing you to savor your own intelligence."

"You're a most unusual man. What are you exactly?"

"You mean what do I do?"

"Yes."

"I'm a private enquiry agent."

"A detective!"

I nodded. I could feel her gaze on me.

"Would you like a job?" Her voice was eager.

"I've got one," I said drily.

"But this is important!" she said urgently.

I could have laughed aloud.

"I'm sure it is," I said.

"I'll pay you well!"

"Uh-huh."

"And it will be interesting for you. I want you to find Helen Seferis!"

I grinned at her.

"Listen, darling," I said gently, "shall we talk about it tomorrow?"

"And tonight?"

"Tonight," I said, "is for us." I lit myself a cigarette. She took it from my lips.

"I think you're a most immoral man, " Nadya said.

Although it is a bachelor flat, it has no Spartan qualities. I refer of course to my own little flat off Mayfair, a district in which a beautiful woman causes little comment. It has five rooms, a kitchen and a bathroom, made over as follows. In the first place, there is my own bedroom where I sleep when I sleep alone. That is rather a bare room, with a modern bed, a dressing table, fitted wardrobes. Three original nudes by Degas line the walls.

The second room is my guest bedroom—a conventional room, furnished in white pine, comfortable, commodious, with one large Renoir. If it is true, as it is reported to be true, that Renoir painted only pregnant nudes—the pregnancy is registered, they say, in the eyes—then my choice of a painting was justified, for some of my friends are respectably married, and in that room, with that picture on the wall, they can retire with a praiseworthy lust to procreate themselves.

The third room is my study—desk, books, anglepoised lamp, oak furniture, and etchings by Goya.

Thus I am surrounded by crime; I am, as it were, in my element. The fourth room is my sitting room—lounge, what you will—which is where, regardless of their sex and purposes, all my guests come initially, to be, as it were, graded, the pictures here being Modigliani at his most sensual, an acid test, I feel, of the proclivities of those who drink Martinis or whatever is to their taste on the comfortable divans. The fifth room is, without doubt, the *pièce de la résistance*. Not everyone is allowed a glimpse of this room, a room, by the way, in which the pretensions of art are never exhibited, the glass room. Many, as the saying goes, were called to the sitting room, but few were chosen for the glass room. I talk in the past tense. I really don't know why, for I still own my little Mayfair flat and I have no doubt that it will serve in the future as it has in the past, as a kind of selection station and delightful hatchery.

Nadya walked into the sitting room like a goddess. I couldn't remember seeing a more beautiful woman in that background. Before she had even removed her wrap she had crossed the room to one of the Modigliani nudes and had uttered a little cry of delight.

"What a beautiful painting," she exclaimed. "It looks just like me!"

"Unfortunately, I haven't had the pleasure of making the comparison," I said with a smile.

She laughed softly. "Help me off with my wrap," she said.

I hastened to her assistance.

She sat crosslegged on the divan while I fixed the drinks. When I returned with her glass she had settled back against the cushions, her body under the beautiful white dress languorous and soft. I shaded the lamp and sat down close to her.

39

"Music?"

"I'd love music," she said.

It was a mere coincidence that I selected a little pile of Arab records and placed them on the plate of the radio-gram. The small quavering voice of an Arab woman suddenly cut into the silence.

"This is Arab music!"

"Yes, don't you like it?"

"Oh, yes, very much! That's where Helen is. She's somewhere in Algeria."

"Helen Seferis," I said, enunciating the name slowly. "It's a Greek name, isn't it?"

"I suppose it is, but she wasn't Greek."

"Wasn't? You believe she's dead then?"

"I have no idea," Nadya said softly. "It's not unlikely...but I thought we were going to leave all that for tomorrow?"

"So we were!" I laughed. "And meanwhile..." I left my sentence unfinished and sat down beside her on the divan. At that moment, the Arab woman's voice broke out harshly from the musical accompaniment, and we said nothing until the instruments, as though hypnotized by the thick lust in the woman's voice, rose and engulfed her before all was silent in a crash of percussion.

We were looking at one another.

"You're quite handsome," she said playfully.

"And you're quite beautiful," I replied.

"Do you believe," said Nadya, smiling, "in love at first sight? Or, at least lust at first sight."

"I do tonight," I responded with a wink.

The arm of the radio-gram clicked over and the music came again.

Her body was warm and of a smooth firm resiliency under the lustrous white silk of her dress. Sometimes, with the pressure of my hand, I felt the

40

soft material come apart from that more subtle, that more ambiguous smoothness which slipped gently away under my fingertips. She reclined backwards on the cushions, as yet entirely unruffled. But at the same time her body seemed to exude that heavy, abandoned aura of desire, so that while she appeared cool and apparently self-controlled, her body was slow, soft, and exaggeratedly at ease. She was, in her very nature, simply a sexual animal.

My lips kissed at the smooth perfection of her eyelids, delicate as shells and then, travelling lower over the soft hollow of her cheek, alighted on the smooth olive skin of her neck. Her breathing came more heavily, causing her firm breasts to rise tremulously under the silky fabric, while the muscles of her abdomen molded themselves under my forearm. I guided my hand around and over the superb silk-clung sweep of her buttocks—pale golden orbs, quite flawless, whose silhouette I could already see in my imagination, tilted this way and that, in every exotic posture, for, when they were finally naked, rising upwards or sideways from her garb, they would shed their sable forms in every mirror of my inner sanctum, the glass room, exposed in all their secrets in the tinted mirrors, of amethyst, saffron, topaz, jade, or tawny amber, and, in the ordinary mirrors, that pearly bare skin would appear off-white, muddy, as though smoke seeped beneath its surfaces.

I was in no hurry. I wished to excite her passion slowly, to see each marvel unveiled in time, to feel her scented heat rise gradually to me through the delicate fabrics which shrouded her nakedness.

The Arab woman sobbed breathlessly through a series of half and quarter notes.

Nadya closed her eyes then, and her soft body rippled under the dress with an already pressing impatience. Nothing of her beautiful torso was visible save the broad 'V' at her neck and the beginnings, the outer lippings of breasts which furrowed downward beneath the bodice of her dress. I turned her on her side and cradled her head in my arm, teasing with the fingers of my other hand the soft wisps of blue-black hair at the nape of her neck. The smooth skin of her back already exuded a moistness which caused the skin to take on the texture of chalk. It was just like that. It was as though I were tracing with my finger-tips the surface of a broad slab of chalk, for, on raising my fingers, I felt a kind of pollen, an accumulation of moist dust, at the pores. The palm of my hand slid downward, all feeling there in touch, in the mute and sullen contact strung between our skins, and all motivation, for my fingers soon alighted on the hooks at the back of her dress and, when they were undone, my hand moved eagerly down the graceful sweep of her spine to the very brink of the ravine where her quivering lobes met. At that point I desisted, but gently, and with small finger-motions, so as not to disturb the continuity of the caress.

The husky voice of the Arab woman caused my hand to quiver and my groin to tighten as—for the upper part of the dress was now loose—I lifted the bodice gently from off her breasts.

The brassière, as I had suspected, was built into the dress itself. And thus in one movement the wonderful pale flower of her upper torso was bared. The fragrance of the arching breasts was almost overpowering. Nervous, opaque, slightly lemonish, with an almost silvery surface, due in part to the pin-prick sweat of her excitement and in part to the naturally sombre colour of her skin, her breasts were studded with two magnificent black nipples, created like the edges of rain-soft grounded leaves and giving the impression of being rooted deeply in the full honey-colored convexities of her flesh. They, and the supple line of her belly—that part of it at least which was already disclosed—had an almost leopard-like quality about them, the honey-colored glint of the breasts and the startling black tip of her strong and upheld tits. They had been dusted with a delicate scent, and that artifice, threaded with the pervasive sweetness of her own passionate flesh, drew my lips downward, at first into the smooth and downy valley between them and then, inexorably, my mouth loosening in sensuality, over one of the sudden rubbery stigmatae of her womanhood. As my mouth became greedy, her slender palms alighted at my temples, coaxing my head downward, inciting me to ravish her; to take the sweet dark chocolate nipple buds deep into the wetness of my mouth and gently, then more firmly, tug them inward with a swishing motion and simultaneously further titillate them by sweeping my tongue across the stiffened buds, slapping them lightly with licks.

Meanwhile, in response to my own rising passion, the fingers of my right hand moved upwards over the seam of one of her sheer nylon stockings and tripped at its extreme edge on to the soft field of her upper thigh. Her panties were as delicate as cobwebs, and their frail substanceless filaments only added to the attraction of the hot, thick, sensuous seams of flesh whose presence under the silky short hairs registered itself in a gradual, almost soapy emission at my fingertips. The smell of sex boiled between her legs and the aroma wafted its way to my nostrils.

Her buttocks twitched and her body arched backwards. She sighed a long, sensual sigh.

"Let me take my dress off," she whispered urgently. I could hardly bring my head away from her breasts. I wanted to keep them trapped in the warmth of my mouth, captive to my tongue and gently gnawing teeth. I wanted to swallow the glorious globes whole, to take the flesh deep into my throat and then to let them go, and lick the little buds lightly until she truly, truly begged for all I could offer to calm the fire in her belly.

But finally I pushed myself up into an upright position and looked at her. She was like some beautiful mythological creature, woman from the waist up, shellfish from the waist down, for the corrugations of her white silk dress, in which buttocks, thighs and cunt were buried, encased her like a shell. I had often wondered at the significance of such mythological creatures as mermaids. At that moment, watching the beautiful honey-colored coil of her upper torso, seeing it, for all its tawny magnificence with its proud tar black nipples, the faint shade of blue-black hair at the armpits, the cascade of it at her oval face, seeing it truncated suddenly, fixed, as it were, in a hard white shell, it struck me suddenly that the horror of mermaids lay in their limitless powers of seductions and in their inability to give sexual satisfaction. No wonder the mariner feared them. Locked fast against their soft breasts his loins nevertheless would thrash abortively against the ungiving belly of a fish.

I longed to spread my mermaid wide apart down there and bury myself in her flesh. But first, I stood up, found a cigarette and lit it.

Nadya, meanwhile, had stepped out of her dress and was removing her gauze-like underclothes. Glancing at the finest of the Modigliani nudes, I realized immediately that Nadya's delighted remark had been no idle boast. On the contrary, she was more beautiful than any painting could have been. Her body seemed to contain all symmetries and every distortion of which an artist is capable. She was vulgar and ravishing. She was superb and lewd. Her buttocks were a shapeless mass of sex and the most perfectly spheroid I had ever seen. Her cunt was a pussy animal, lithe as a goddess's, clean-cut and more delicate than the lips of a child. As she turned towards me, her dark nylon stockings still on and making lips of the soft flesh of her upper thighs, held there by two thin black thongs gathered at her waist by a soft ribbon of silk, I felt like falling down on my knees to worship her.

She raised one thigh as a horse might. "Do you want me to take these off?" she said. "Mario preferred me to keep them on."

It was like being confronted with an impossibly good menu, one on which there appear such alternative succulent dishes, dishes probably of equal merit such as one finds it impossible to choose without the feeling of having missed out on something irretrievably. Thus, and sadly, I shook my head in indecision.

She laughed at my predicament.

"Are you going to fuck me or aren't you?" she said roguishly.

That brought me back to my senses. I smiled.

"Not here!" I said quickly. "The glass room! You've never seen anything like the glass room!"

With that, I took her hand and led her through a door into my chamber of pleasures. As soon as we were inside, Nadya's lissome body was flung back at us from all directions, delicately tinted by a hundred square yards of skillfully treated glass.

She stood for a moment, gazing in all directions.

"What do you think of it?"

"Oh, it's wonderful! It's wonderful!" she said.

"From more than one point of view!" I said, lifting her naked body into my arms.

I set her down on the bed, and quickly joined her.

Nadya reached for me, eager to consummate the passion that had been building between us all evening. I allowed my hands and lips to roam about her body, free at last to do with her as I wished. Reflections of our activities danced all about us on the walls of my special room. Oddly, this did not make us feel self-conscious, but rather, it increased our sense of liberation. It was as if the two of us upon this bed were the only things that mattered, or had ever mattered, and that the rest of the world was simply a dream from which we had suddenly awakened.

For a moment, I lay beside her and simply gazed into those wild, dark eyes. I could smell the sex oozing from her and was anxious to see if the cunt of my fantasies was the same as the one between those olive green legs.

"Spread yourself wide open for me," I whispered in her ear. "Let me see that gorgeous cunt, in all the colors and reflections of the mirrors."

She looked at me with a sexy smile and then, opening her still-stockinged legs wide, she put her hands down to the cunt lips and spread them, and there before my eyes was a pussy feast of the dark, lithe, spectacular cunt folds I had dreamed and now they would blossom right before my eyes.

First, I kissed the nearly-black nipple, and sucked on the hardened bud, stirring deep desire in her lower parts. I kissed the titties, then the smooth flat belly and honey skin and worked my way over the blue-black pussy hairs to her wide open snatch. I kissed it, gently, and felt and saw it swell as blood rushed to her cunt lips with the pleasure response of sex.

She moaned. "Fuck me, please," she begged. "Oh, please, fuck me."

My cock was hard, like a piece of wood, and I was

ready to get deep inside that gorgeous dark hole. I wanted to be consumed by the blossoming cunt petals as I pounded my prick into the depths of her. But first, the most delicious of tortures—a tongue flick to the clit.

She arched her back and pressed her pussy forward as I flicked my tongue this way and that, and she moaned in low animal wails. "Oh please, suck it at least, don't tease me so," she pleaded. "Oh, suck my clit, suck the come out of me, please, suck it now."

I ignored her, knowing that the pleasure I bestowed upon her was greater than even she knew yet and I would bring her to the edge of climax and then give her all she wanted.

Her cunt was very juicy and wet, so I slipped a finger in as I flicked my tongue across her clit. This made her gyrate even faster, and press her pussy forward to impale her horny cunt on my finger.

The ass and hips and thighs moved up and down as I licked her, and now there was a natural rhythm occurring that told me she was close to the edge.

"Now you can have the big prize," I promised. I took off my trousers and prepared to enter her.

She wriggled beneath me as I poised the head of my manhood at the gateway to her cunt. I slipped it toward the opening. "Oh, yes," she squealed with delight, "Oh yes, fuck me, that's it, fuck me now, baby, I want some cock. Gimme, gimme. Do it."

She was wild, absolutely transformed into an animal, and thus I pressed in and slid the length of myself into the deep dark hole of my desires, and we fucked.

The motions were reserved, at first, and then we picked up the beat to the tune of the Arab lady wailing in the background, and my cock was getting drawn deep into her womb by the squeezing, then pulling in of her cunt muscles.

"I'm going to come," she was panting, "you come too, come inside me, squirt your juice in me."

I started to fuck her fiercely, pummel her, and press myself to the very hilt. My balls flapped against her butt as she pressed up to meet my thrusts.

Both of us panted and breathed and sweated like animals as our groins banged against one another in this animal fuck. And finally, as her cunt began to climax, her muscles squeezed around my cock so hard that it brought me to climax also.

I shot a huge stream of jism into that glorious black hole, surrounded by those thin, dark cunt petals, and then I lay on top of her as all the come drained into her cunt and began to drip from her cunt to the bed.

"There's just one more thing I have to do," I said. With that, I bent down between her legs and lapped the combined juices from the smooth olive skin. Shortly thereafter, we fell asleep in one another's arms. Well at least she was safe—and I in fact, was doing my job by protecting her!

Chapter 3

"Good afternoon," Laura said.

"Don't be funny."

"I'm not. It is precisely two minutes past twelve."

"The hell it it!"

"You've missed four appointments, and Lord Grisskillin called three times during the morning."

"What the hell did he want!"

"It appears that some charge of his didn't return to her hotel last night. He said you were supposed to be looking after her. I told him you probably were."

"How clever of you!"

I sprawled down behind my desk and lit a cigarette.

"He wasn't satisfied," Laura said.

"Who wasn't satisfied?"

"Lord Grisskillin. He said that if she didn't turn up by noon he was going to call in Scotland Yard."

"And what did you say?"

"I said I didn't think it would be necessary. I asked him not to do so until he heard from you."

"Bloody old ass! What did he say then?"

"He said he'd give you until noon, that if you hadn't contacted him by then he was going to call in the police."

"What the hell are you waiting for then! Get him on the line at once!"

"I've already put in the call. The line's busy. The exchange is going to ring back."

"My God!"

"Your God," said Laura, "is not a miracle-worker. He's got one lecherous eye and its range of vision is singularly limited."

"Sure," I said, "he's a Cyclops."

But before Laura had time to reply the telephone rang.

"Henry Park?"

An affirmation was stuttered from the other end of the wire.

"Lord Grisskillin? Just a moment, sir. Mr. Harvest will speak to you now."

I lurched over and grabbed the telephone.

"Hello?…Yes, of course it's me…Who the hell did you think it was!"

"Where is she, you fool? Did you know she didn't return to her hotel last night?"

"Of course I knew! Remember, she has the morals of a tomcat?…Yes, quite safe…I didn't leave her side all night."

"Indeed!"

"What I mean is, I was within calling distance."

"I must say you express yourself very badly!"

"Look, she's all right, do you hear? Nothing's going to happen to her. Now, will you leave the job to me?"

The receiver clicked at the other end.

"The old fool's cut me off!"

"He was a friend of your mother," Laura said sweetly.

"That remark is neither funny nor instructive," I said, replacing the receiver. I returned to my own desk and began to doodle on a memo pad.

"Unusual for you to operate at calling distance, isn't it?" Laura said with a smile.

"I have no idea what you mean," I replied.

"I thought your maximum distance was the thickness of 52 gauge nylon," said Laura.

"Perhaps I'm dull this morning, but I don't appreciate your humor."

"You look as though you hadn't slept for a week."

"It's often difficult for a detective to get sleep," I said.

"You're in bed often enough, God knows."

"Your God's knowledge," I said, pleased at last to be able to think of a reply, "is singularly limited—like my God's vision, indeed. She uses the word 'know' only in the biblical sense."

"If I remember rightly, that was your line when you seduced me," said Laura drily. "You said you wanted to get to know me!"

"How silly of you to take what people say seriously! I merely nurtured a seed that already existed."

"I think you're horrible," Laura said. "You make me sound like some kind of vegetable!"

"Precisely," I said. "A plant rather than a vegetable. All beautiful women are like plants."

"Oh!" Laura's tone was uncertain. "You mean it as a compliment then?"

"Of course!"

"And what about Miss Pamandari? Is she a plant too?"

"Yes…she's some kind of hothouse orchid. You, on the other hand, are a tulip."

"You mean I'm plebeian!"

"Not at all. I see no reason to introduce that kind of concept into the present discussion."

Laura was silent for a moment. I had been dabbling with a verse on the memo pad.

"Here," I said, "what do you think of this? It's poetry!"

Laura looked at me with a faint smile on her lovely lips,

I read:

> Love (what mothers call infatuation)
> is a cosmic vibration
> often immoderate
> like hate.
> It lives in the thighs
> is consummate
> in beds, fields, cinemas or pig sties,
> according to mood, heat and opportunity…

"What do you think of that!"

"I think," said Laura slowly, "that you can accomplish more variations on a single theme than any other man I know. On the other hand, I think it's a great pity that you can't invent another theme."

"There isn't one," I said with a smile.

"That," said Laura, "is what I meant about the limits of your vision."

"And that," I replied, "is what I meant about the limits of your knowledge."

"I don't see much point in further discussion," Laura said.

"Nor do I. I'm going out for lunch now. I may not be back this afternoon."

"I don't think there's much doubt about it, do you?" said Laura, fixing me with a cold, green-eyed stare.

"You promised to listen, Anthony!"

"How do you expect me to be interested in another woman at this moment?" I answered with a smile.

"If you knew Helen you'd soon cool down," Nadya said drily.

She took a sip of her coffee and continued: "And if you don't listen, you'll never have a chance of seeing her. She may be being murdered at this very moment."

"All right," I said in a resigned tone of voice, "you tell me. Who exactly is Helen Seferis?"

"She is a friend of my father's," Nadya said, and more quietly, "my friend too. I fell in love with a young American on the boat coming from Bombay and Helen ran off with him at Marseilles."

"I thought you said she was a friend of yours!"

"She is. She knew my father wouldn't approve of Devlin. She thought I might do something silly, like getting married to him. So she eloped with him herself and took him to Monte Carlo."

"And now they're in Algeria?"

"She is, but he isn't. He's dead. He lost all his money in Monte Carlo and committed suicide. After that, Helen was kidnapped by an Arab and sold, I think to a brothel, and that's all we know."

"Where did you get your information?"

"Her diary was found. I've brought a copy of it along with me. You must read it, and then you must go and find her."

"Do the French police know?"

"It was they who passed on the information. They can't find her and my father has had a firm of private detectives in Algeria for more than three months. I had a letter from him last week. He has decided to give up the search."

"And you want me to have a shot at it?"

"I'll pay you what you ask."

"I can't promise. I have a lot of work here. You'd better let me take a look at the diary."

She passed over a typed manuscript of two hundred or more pages. I was somewhat put out by its length.

"It's more like a book," I said. "What is it, her life story?"

"Read it and see," said Nadya with a smile.

I looked at my watch.

"I'll go to my club," I said. "I'll meet you back here in the cocktail bar at five."

"You'll give me your decision then?"

"If possible. But you must remember, Nadya, that a great number of people have been looking for her for a long time already. The scent is almost dead. Even if I decide to go, I may not succeed."

"I think you will," Nadya replied. "Sometimes I can't understand myself. You're the first man who has really interested me since Devlin, and now I'm sending you away, and to Helen of all people!"

"What do you think I am, a conditioned reflex!"

"You won't want to be anything else when you see Helen," said Nadya in her husky voice.

I sat back in the reading room of my club near St. James Place. On my knees lay the manuscript, still unopened. Frankly, told without detail, the story sounded phony. The white slave racket is a dangerous one and the slavers don't go out of their way to choose the female acquaintances of important men like Mr. Pamandari. I gathered from Grisskillin's concern about Nadya that Mr. Pamandari was the kind of man who made and unseated governments. If you're a wise criminal, you don't upset men like that. If necessary, they'll start a war to have your skin. No. The usual cargo was a cargo of minnows: waitresses, pantry maids, girls who come up from the country to find 'exciting' employment, neurotic women who will marry strange men in strange towns and fly by night without a word to their acquaintances.

That was point number one. This is my usual procedure. I approach all my problems in this way. I like to get a general picture before I lose myself in a morass of relevant and irrelevant details.

Secondly, it seemed to me damned strange to say the least of it that the French police, who are experts in these kinds of things, had been unable to locate the missing woman's whereabouts.

Thirdly, any firm of private detectives employed by a man like Mr. Pamandari would be experts, would be assured from the beginning of all the help that the police could give them, and were unlikely to come up with something after three month's investigation.

Thus, my attitude as I opened the manuscript was one of polite disbelief.

It began with a letter from one French officer to another which reported the abduction of Miss Seferis by a Sheikh X, and of the discovery of the manuscript (the diary) on the person of an Arab arrested in connection with a theft.

The Sheikh was an important man in French Algeria. That would account for the difficulty of the search.

I read the letter quickly, turned the page, and was at once caught up in the hothouse quality of the woman's prose:

"It is dark where I am lying, alone, in a tent, on a few sheepskins that they provided for me. They have taken my clothes away from me and have given me the clothes of an Arab woman..."

It was a quarter to five when I finally closed the folder. There was no longer any doubt in my mind that I would go to Algeria. The woman who was created in the pages of the diary, rising like a pale flower out of a nightmare, had captivated me. I realized then that from the day I read the manuscript, until the day I would hold her in my arms, my life could have only one purpose. Compared to Helen Seferis, Nadya was merely a wonderfully sensual child, and Laura, whom, in spite of our quarrels, I had still suspected I would marry, became a civilized creature whose primal nature was lost, irrevocably, beneath the veneer of manners which she had cultivated in the face of social life.

And yet I had no idea what she looked like!

She was blonde according to Nadya. Her own descriptions of herself in the diary required confirmation—long white flanks, the breasts of a goddess, the belly and sex of an enchantress.

I stubbed my cigarette, put the manuscript carefully in my briefcase, and took a taxi to meet Nadya.

In spite of its length, the facts I derived from the manuscript were surprisingly few.

After the suicide of Devlin she had left on the yacht of Sheikh X for Algiers. She was transported quickly from that city to Blida, where they stayed with a friend of her abductor. From Blida, still unaware of her new lover's intentions, she had consented to a trip in the desert, expecting to rejoin Nadya in Paris in about a fortnight. About a week later, they had travelled by camel for three days, and

Youssef, as she referred to him here, watched her being raped by two of the camel men and then left with part of the caravan.

It wasn't clear as to whether the Sheikh set it up for his viewing pleasure, or he happened upon it and just did not care to stop it. But basically she was in a tent, her wrists were tied, and one camel man spread the honey-milk legs of Helen Seferis and licked the honey between them and the other forced her to suck on his cock, which was extraordinarily huge—about eleven inches.

The one who started by licking her pussy then pulled himself over her and inserted himself. His cock was relatively small and she took it with little fanfare. But his special twist was to bite and abuse her breasts while he fucked and this caused black and blue marks after the fact and—she admitted—an exotic sensation while it was going on.

The Sheikh apparently watched the first man eat, fuck and bite the nipples of Helen Seferis while she was forced to suck the cock of the other man. When the first camel man came, the other ordered him to get a warm cloth to wiped the come away. This was done. The man with the large cock then pulled his huge, hard, purple-headed monster of a cock from her mouth—where the sheer size alone was nearly choking her as she sucked him between pretty pink lips—and was ready to fuck her.

To accommodate his huge wong, she had to be propped up on a pillow. He got on top of her, and pressed forward. The Sheikh, and the other man who had just fucked her, watched with great interest to see how far the man with the huge cock could get himself into the tight little pink-lipped quim. He was about half in when she called out, begging him to take it easy. Because the cock, aside from being so long, was about one and a half inches in diameter—it was thick and he was intent on fucking her with all of it.

She wriggled, but it got her nowhere. Her hands were still tied, her legs were up in the air, her ass was raised by the pillow, and the camel man with the huge cock was not three quarters in and he began pumping her.

The huge cock filled the walls of her cunt entirely, and stretched both the lips and the inner cunt apart, but the longer he stayed in the more used to it she became and soon she was able to allow him all the way in without straining to block him, and then getting sore as a result.

The Sheikh watched this intently, with great interest since he himself had not a very large cock. But soon the camel man with the big penis started fucking very hard and fast and was on the verge of coming. He pumped himself deeply into Helen, who gritted her teeth but took him deeply into her cunthole, and when he came, he pulled out to show his jealous observers there were great gads of white, pearly come exploding from his cock, all over Helen's flat, pink belly and sweet, golden pubic hair. He won a round of applause for his action; she on the other hand, was just left there, his come drying up on her legs and belly.

From that point onwards there was no indication of her whereabouts—an occasional unnamed watering hole, an occasional glimpse of white houses, of marketplaces, of minarets, all anonymous.

Miss Seferis, in her writings, seemed to be concerned with little other than her sexuality.

The only other useful information was contained in the second letter which passed between the two French colonial officers. The facts to be derived from a perusal of that letter were as follows:

(1) Helen Seferis had been sold to a brothel, the identity of which was unknown.

(2) Mr. Pamandari's long arm had already taken vengeance upon the perpetrator of the abduction. Sheikh X had been mysteriously assassinated.

(3) The firm of private detectives had at least begun their work with confidence, even if now they had reached a dead end in investigations.

(4) Doubtless because of Mr. Pamandari's influence, the French President himself had interested himself in the matter.

(5) But all this to no avail. Her whereabouts were still unknown.

I could expect no further information until I arrived in Algeria.

Present time has a color, an odor, a texture, to which neither memory nor anticipation can attain. Thus, for the most part, being a sensualist rather than a sentimentalist, and as Algeria was as yet a long way off, I returned like a bee to my flower—the olive-skinned, dark-haired Nadya, whose legs so easily spread for me and whose cunt embraced my swollen member with a warm, loving receptacle. After meeting Nadya at the cocktail bar, as planned, I was eager to bring her back to the glass room for a night of pleasure; my passion was inspired by the writings of Helen Seferis.

She stood there, a sultry vixen whose dark features, eyes and hair were a far throw from what I imagined Helen Seferis to look like.

The suave rise of her breasts flashed back at me from all directions. She was standing in the center of the glass room, her clean-cut figure young and smooth as polished stone, and she was laughing at the various colored reflections of herself. The flexions of her muscles were superb, the masses and shades of them blending subtly with the magnificent curve of her torso. When she flexed her toes, her body arched upwards to the twin caps of her prominent dark nipples, while her gleaming black hair, loose now, lay like a stranded veil on the perfect mellow globes of her poised buttocks whose delicate tremor suggested that in them resided the nexus, the vital fulcrum, of all her sensitive nerve endings. Their motion was almost non-motion, resembling more than anything else the gleaming spiral movement of a metal top, whose motion is on another axis, a spinning top which, from one point of view, is entirely at rest, for their delicate balance gave one the impression of something which congeals or, better, of something utterly dynamic momentarily caught in voluptuous static form. Her mound, the bud of her love, was like a soft wet paintbrush set at the meeting of her generous thighs. She turned, still studying herself, and faced me. Her skin rippled with smooth muscle as she moved toward me.

"Must I really come as far as Paris with you?"

Her sudden turn brought her front into prominence.

"Yes," I replied. "Otherwise I can't go."

"You haven't told me why!"

She ran her hand down over the pointed jut of her breast to the quivering line of her belly, tense in her risen position, and lower, arching across the gleaming groove of her body's centre on to her right thigh. It rested there, like a wilted flower.

"I don't intend to," I said with a smile. "If you'll come as far as Paris and stay for at least a month, I shall go to North Africa. Otherwise, the answer is no. And if I hear you've set foot in England while I am away, I'll call the whole thing off, do you understand?"

"But I've been in Paris!" Nadya said in a spoilt voice. "I want to stay in London."

"You can't."

"Why can't I!"

"Because I say so," I said quietly. "Those are my terms. Take them or leave them. You can go to Rome or Berlin or anywhere else you want, but you must leave this country. And if you don't, I shan't."

She giggled. "Oh, all right. I believe you're jealous!"

Really, I don't think it mattered to her in the slightest. She was merely making conversation while she admired herself, and incidentally held my attention at the same time. Nadya adored an audience, especially if she was the naked center of attention. In that way she reminded me of Sybil, a girl I used to know. Sybil Batterram was the greatest exhibitionist I ever knew. She was the wife of one of my early clients who wanted his wife tailed for a month so that he could have an affair safely with another woman. The idea was that if she got within five minutes of the other woman's flat, he, who was already there, should be telephoned immediately. It turned out to be a very profitable business, because the very next morning Sybil herself turned up at my office and wanted to speak to me confidentially. I assured her that everything she said to me would be treated with the utmost confidence.

Sybil wanted her husband tailed because she too had some secret lusts to fulfill. She frankly admitted to me that for many years she had nursed a private passion that she had never before spoken of to a living soul. I inclined my head sympathetically. For her purposes, she had to be sure that her husband wouldn't interrupt her in what she called 'the satiation of this silly lust of mine.' She wished to be witnessed in adultery without running the inevitable risk of her husband finding out, which could result in divorce. She wished, in short, to be taken by a man who was not her husband in front of a third party, or preferably, several parties, and to capture it all on film. She wanted to make sure her supporting cast was utterly trustworthy. A friend of mine had mentioned my name to her. He had told her that I was discreet, trustworthy, and at the same time a cultivated connoisseur of delicate lusts. Thus, here she was, seeking my counsel.

I made no bones about the fact that her little spectacle interested me greatly. "Am I to understand that I was to choose not only the supporting cast but the male lead as well?" I asked her.

"Naturally!" she said with a small smile. "Only he must be about your size, with your good looks, very lustful, and the epitome of discretion. You understand?"

"Indeed, madam," I said slowly, "and with your permission, I'd like to submit myself to play the role!"

"What a delightful man you are Mr. Harvest! That would be most satisfactory!"

"The pleasure, I assure you, will be mine. As for the details, allow me to arrange them. I will see that your husband is occupied elsewhere. I shall telephone you after dinner tonight."

I repeat, I have never again met a woman so avid of exhibiting her lusts. She wished to engrave them on the world's memory. She was a kind of kinky artist, a sort of lustful ecdysiast. On the outside, in demeanor and comportment, she would not have looked out of place shaking hands with a vicar in the portals of a church. But naked, stripped of her discretions, she would have turned a palace into a brothel.

Inside her luxurious flat, she insisted on arranging everything. One member of the supporting cast was to handle the movie camera, another was to control the microphone, my friend John Devins, the third—for I had brought three confederates, members of a little circle of mine, two women and a man—was to make himself an obvious witness, to leer pruriently and shout coarse remarks, things like "spread yourself wide open so I can have a peek." This was what Sybil requested.

She was a woman who knew exactly what she wanted. "Now," she said, "we must begin at the beginning. You and I, Mr. Harvest, will sit on the bed, opposite the camera and you will begin by making improper advances to me. You will put your hand on my knee, raise my skirt. At that point," she said to Gwen, the camera operator, "the camera lens should be lowered to take in my thighs. I shall kick a little, pretending to resist—that can be very artful. I want to get into my movement that kind of impotent reluctance that long grass has in a strong wind, you know what I mean? And then you, Mr. Harvest, must tear my nylon stockings off, tear, do you understand?"

I nodded in admiration.

"The more I kick," she continued gaily, "the more my private parts will be exposed. It should be zoomed up close to the very pink of the skin, focused on every fold and drop of wetness. At this point, the camera should be very close. I shall make all sorts of noises, and those and all the other noises, those of the witnesses, for example, will be recorded. You, Mr. Harvest, must be content with baring the lower part of me to begin with. Tear my panties clear off as well. Rip them off as though you were righteously indignant about them. Toss me, roughly, on to the carpet. And demonstrate an animal desire by pawing at the rest of my clothes. We shan't get completely in the raw until the second wicket, so to speak." She paused. "Has everyone got the picture?"

We all nodded.

"Well," the inventive Sybil continued, "there's just one more point before we begin. Whoever is operating the microphone..."

"Lucy," I said helpfully.

"Well, Lucy, you have another job. Over there on that table, you will notice there are two gramophones. The one on the right is an automatic one. After you've switched it on, you don't need to pay any attention to it. It will fill in with background music throughout the course of the whole thing. But the other one is important. The record on it is a reproduction of the noise an express train makes as it enters a tunnel, you know that rather ghostly high pitched hoot? Well, at the moment at which Mr. Harvest moves in to penetrate me, I want you to play that record. Allow three or four such hoots until Mr. Harvest is completely embedded in the depths of me, and then turn the record over, quickly, you understand, because we want to get the full benefit of what's on the other side—this is the reproduction of noises recorded in a pig sty at feeding time. It's a fiendishly erotic sound to fuck by! The pigs, the soft music from the other gramophone, and our own animal grunts and noises, should harmonize well together."

At this point, the first set of stage instructions ceased.

"Did you think up all this yourself, Mrs. Batterram?" Gwen asked in an admiring voice.

"I've had hot pants for it for over five years!" replied Sybil with a small laugh. "The actual details came to me gradually over a period of time, of course. Actually during various connections with my husband. To make connection with him at all tolerable, I was forced to fantasize a great deal."

"I'd like to try it myself, some time," Gwen said enviously.

"Oh, but you will, my dear," said the redoubtable Mrs. Batterram. "We shall have heaps of opportunities to do all sorts of things in the future. But tonight is mine. It's my début. At last, it's about to happen!"

"All set?" I said. "Everyone to his position!"

"The arc lights are switched on next to the camera lead," said Sybil as she nestled softly back on the couch, her black leather skirt wrinkled and already above her pretty knees. "Do you think you could take me now, Mr. Harvest?" she said in a soft tantalizing voice.

"I am already your devoted slave," I said, placing a tentative hand on the warm heavy weight of her right thigh.

I tore off her black nylons, as promised and then ripped off her panties, per her request, and she pretended to fight. But as she kicked her legs in mock resistance my eyes feasted hungrily upon a luscious bush of brown cunt fuzz which delicately covered the beautifully pink and fleshy cunt lips that rested between her long, trim legs.

She kicked and grunted as if trying to get away, I pulled her closer to me by the hips and roughly spread open her legs so as to get a much better look at the cunt which was now to be mine for the taking.

Lucy, the camera person, zoomed in. And John, the voyeur, stood close by, oogled the inner pussy lips that lay spread before me, and, as promised, began to recite obscenities at Sybil.

"Open your cunt, bitch, and let me see the deep pink recess between your legs," he was saying. "Let me see how wet you are. Yum, I can almost taste the salty pussy juices from between your legs."

On that note, I took one lone, middle finger and wiggled it around the opening of her slit. She pretended to resist and yet purposefully, in that motion, impaled her cunt upon the finger and I could feel immediately this wild, wet, juicy inner cunt that I longed to stick my own, now-throbbing member into.

She squirmed with pleasure, as she fought her impulses to succumb, so she could keep fighting for the sake of the camera. She started to grunt so, for effect, I grabbed one of the ripped nylons and gagged her. Her eyes became alight with pure lust when I did this.

John, too, was getting sexually agitated by the sight of the pink prettiness that poked out from between her milky thighs and as he berated her with obscenities—"Yes, cunt, let me see more of you, I'd like to fuck you, bitch." I noticed him taking off his pants and whipping out his large, swollen cock which he began to jerk off in front of us all.

Meanwhile, Sybil, gagged and staring at John jerking off, and spreading her legs so wide that the camera was practically inside her pussy, began to gyrate her hips upward, as if she were fucking into the air. I got up, hastily stepped out of my shirt and trousers, and got back on the bed with her, my knees now kneeling between hers. I looked at her, and ungagged her.

"Now, will you stop resisting," I asked, playing the mock rapist. "Will you stop fighting it; you know you want it. Tell me how much you want it. Tell it to the camera, and to the microphone, so the whole world will know what you want to have stuck up between those pretty white thighs and into the wet little cunt of yours."

She sat up partially, ripped off her sweater and bra, and exposed a pair of apple-perfect titties with pretty pink nipple buds and a nice handful of tit flesh. She grabbed hold of them herself, and began squeezing, and then she hiked her leather skirt all the way up to her waist and ran one finger down the length of her cunt.

She spread herself open with the fingers of one hand."

"Zoom the camera down here," she said, indicating it should come kissing close to her cunt. "Look at my little pink love slash. Drink it in, camera!"

Lucy obliged, and you could tell by the way she was walking toward Sybil that her own cunt was on fire as she zoomed in on Sybil.

"Now, the camera is going to see this cunt get licked with nice, long strokes by Mr. Harvest," she said, shooting a thrill through my cock as she did. "Mr. Harvest, come bring me your hot tongue and eat me."

She now took two hands, spread herself way open, so that I could see the juices of excitement pouring from her as I neared. I bent between her knees and brought my face up to her cunt, conscious to leave some room between my face and her cunt lips so the camera could get a good angle. But once I got close, all I wanted to do was bury my mouth in the mouth between her legs. This I did.

I made my hot tongue flat and fat and licked up and down the shaft of her slit, pressing firmly on her swollen, hard clit as I moved along. She pressed her cunt into my face as I did this. I pressed my tongue down harder.

She was still holding her cunt open for me, so my hands were placed right by the very opening of her sex, whereby I could stretch the tight hole even further apart just as I prepared to stab into her cunt with my tongue.

She was breathing heavy, and all her muscles tightened in anticipation. John and Lucy were panting as well, and when I looked from the corner of my eye I could see that the other woman with us, Claire, was rubbing the round tipped microphone against Lucy's cunt, while Lucy was shakily holding up the camera.

And we were all grunting like pigs, I thought, until I realized that Lucy had put the pig grunting record on.

I dived into Sybil's cunt with great strokes of my tongue and could feel her thighs beginning to shake, to shiver, as she drew near coming from the wild sensations of my tongue lapping at her clit and the two fingers I'd inserted, stabbing deep into the mushy innards of her cunt.

John, you could tell, was near coming, and Lucy swung the camera on him as he started shaking wildly, cursing out to Sybil, "Let your river of come seep out onto Harvest's tongue," as he began to spurt his own juices; they flew over the camera and near Sybil's hair, and inspired me to fuck her now so that I too could unleash some wild explosions into her womb.

"I'm going to fuck you now," I said, as I lifted myself from kneeling between her legs, positioned myself over her, and placed my huge, swollen member at the entrance of her wet, juicy slit.

"Oh, oh, Mr. Harvest, please do, please do, and if I could lick the come off of John's cock as you insert yourself I shall love to get that on film," she said.

John obeyed and walked over to the bed, placing his still hard cock near her mouth; she hungrily grabbed onto it with two hands as she sucked at the juicy come that had spurt out around it, and she pulled him deeply into her mouth just as I jabbed her fully with my cock.

Once I got inside her, I felt like my cock was getting grabbed by a warm, wet, leather-gloved fist that was pulling tightly on my organ. She was tight as a drum, perhaps from lack of fucking with her husband, and she was a delicious fuck.

I was moving furiously, and John, while Sybil sucked him, was watching furiously, keeping to his role of voyeur while she brought his cock back to life again.

I knew I was losing control, that an animal wildness had gripped me, and now I could hear myself truly grunting like the pigs. I was snorting, sniffing, huffing, puffing and so damn near exploding into her velvety insides that I nearly just did it...until I remembered we were in Sybil's fantasy and I was determined to give her a good come.

As I continued to pummel her pussy with my rock hard prick, I grabbed her by the cheeks of her ass and by her hips and hoisted her up against my pole. The way I grabbed her spread her cunt lips even further apart, so I knew now her clit was getting a proper rubbing as I slapped myself into her hole.

She hungrily hoisted herself up to meet my thrusts, and pressed herself onto me. And I could feel her, now, squeezing me with her cunt muscles and dripping delicious droplets of love juice onto my cock, making this quite a lubricated fuck.

"Ohhhhh, ohhhhh, ohhhhh," she was moaning, the pig record oinking in the background, John howling with pleasure as she continued her sucking on and jerking off his cock, and the girls, Claire and Lucy, were now in a 69 whereby they were deliciously gamahuching one another's pretty cunts. The camera, propped up on a ladder, was pointed at our star, Ms. Sybil, and myself, as I plowed into her.

John was the first to come again. Sybil sucked him until his pole was clean of come and she lapped up every ounce of the juice that had splashed on her hand. Then, she put her hands, still sticky with his come, on my face, pulled me to her and kissed me deeply. I could taste the salt of John's come on her tongue but I wanted to kiss her deeply, anyway.

Next, I could hear the moans and groans of both Lucy and Claire as they gyrated their hips into one another's mouths and came, it seemed, simultaneously.

Lucy, who'd gotten so involved with the passionate exchange between her and Claire, having been so heated by the action of Sybil and I on the bed, had forgotten the locomotive record she was to play when I first entered Sybil's wet slash. But she remembered it after she herself had come into the mouth of pretty, blond Claire.

I was fucking Sybil wildly, with absolute abandon, feeling myself on the edge of an orgasm, and pulling her to me tightly, closely, trying to squeeze her orgasm out of her.

She was fucking me back, wildly, her hips foisting themselves upward against my groin, her legs twitching and shaking, her breathing turned into a pant and a snort kind of noise. And suddenly, the locomotive record began to charge through the air just as I was charging through Sybil and the two of us looked at each other in dire, delirious passion and felt our groins melding into one another, and pressing into one another, and fucking one another until the juicy emissions of come began to shoot from us both as our orgasms twitched and ejaculated us into sheer ecstasy.

Her cunt muscles closed so tightly around my rod that they strangled the come out of me; I could feel her own wet, creamy girl-juice oozing onto my cock.

We fell in an exhausted heap and turned to see our voyeur, camerawoman and microphone holder all laying in a heap of cunts, cocks, tits and heads—spent as we were.

"Well my dear," I said to her, the camera still whirring in my head, recording the action and the post-action discussion. "Was it all you had dreamed of?"

"That and more," she said, giving my butt a squeeze. Unfortunately, we had to clean up the place and clear out soon after because I knew her husband would be done with his own afternoon affair shortly after we had completed ours!

That scene was still whirring in my head as I watched Nadya's movements in the glass room. I was snapped back to reality.

It was to be, as we both knew well, our last night together. On the morrow, we should fly together as far as Paris, Nadya would disembark and I should be carried onwards to French North Africa. The thought of that journey and my reason for making it caused a kind of vegetable expansion somewhere in my solar plexus, a kind of 'high' feeling at my loins which reacted enthusiastically toward the carnal immediacy of the present situation.

She had thrown herself on a divan in the centre of the room and was lying with her feet towards me. She lay on her back so that her long opaquely-fleshed legs were thrust forward toward me like twin cylinders, slender at the ankles, thickening towards the calves, caving towards the knees to the flat slabs of her thighs where they thickened at once, gradually and voluptuously, rimmed as it were, where they joined her torso, where the heart-shaped spread of her delicate short hairs began and moved upwards into a faint line

71

on her lower belly. Her body bristled minutely as the muscles turned under short hairs. Below the heart's point, two small pears of flesh were visible, the rest of her superb buttocks being out of sight under her. My eyes travelled upwards over the wonderful form of her body, over the smooth little belly, fitted like a small disc under her rib cage, and the lines of the latter leading suddenly to the magnificent nipple-peaked breasts, above which her delicate shoulders lay, a milky coffee color, and her slender arms, bent at the elbow so that her hands came to meet under the back of her head. At this point she crossed her long legs, folding them about one another, obscuring most of her upper torso and making a perfect heart, deeply indented, of her yellowish ivory buttocks.

I extinguished my cigarette and then I approached and sat near her feet.

I, myself, had been naked for some time. She looked up at me from under lowered eyelids as I sat down, and then slewed round from the waist so that now she lay almost on her side and a thin wisp of her secret hairs grew outward from between her closed thighs like grass from between stones.

"You're quite perfect," I said.

She made no reply, but continued to look at me in a kind of 'withheld' way, not detached, for her dark eyes were heavy with passion. But neither did she seek to encourage my advances.

I hesitated, projecting myself in a kind of emphatic way into that soft readiness which her flesh seemed to symbolize. Its surfaces were underrun by the pregnancy of its desire. What potentialities lurked in that lank yet rounded flesh, bared there, lazily, waiting!

With one hand on her ankle, I leaned forward and brushed my lips against the silky tuft. She laughed delightedly. Automatically, my lips opened to the smooth grassy web and my teeth closed over the tips of the hairs. They tasted lightly of salt, and then sweet. I tugged at them gently. Her buttocks reacted in a slight shudder. As my tongue mingled with the hairs, insistent and cajoling between the flesh of her thighs, she raised her upper knee towards her breast so that the lips of her rosy cleft were pinkly disclosed, the glint of a strange animal in heavy undergrowth. By combing them softly with my tongue, I finally disclosed her sacred mouth, fringed, as it were, by lashes of hair even more delicate than the blackly sweeping eyelashes which veiled her dark eyes. The lips were slightly apart and moist in a kind of helpless lechery, a hot and passionate facsimile of the lips from between which her husky voice, impregnated with the weight of her passion, issued.

Again I hesitated.

She moaned softly. It was a sound at once urgent and small.

As I laid my own lips to them, closed first and tentatively wet, her leaden, lust struck buttocks moved downward like a wall, her olive thighs opening like jaws to contain my whole face. I grasped her firmly at the flesh of her hips and abetted her downward movement so that I shut away all light and sight from myself and was sensitive only at my mouth as I penetrated deeply in the rich seams of her womanhood.

Meanwhile, at my own center, I experienced a gravitational pull. A shutter closed. A key was applied to a lock. There was turning. Our bodies seemed to twist and meet, as her mouth closed over me. She took my cock into her hands, and welcomed it into her mouth. Her tongue rolled over the head, and she delicately sucked me deep into the bowels of her throat while moving her mouth up and down on my pole.

I felt my head pressed between gluttonous weights of her open thighs, the mad foraging at my lips and nose, as though she were trying, spiderlike, by covering me with her mysterious and sweet smelling dew, to draw me within herself, to be pregnant with me, stuffed with me, so that I might feed vitally at the most secret part of her. Meanwhile, as she sucked and sucked at my own pole, I was delirious. My knees closed together, then they spread wide apart; my body bent backwards from the navel in a strong bow of muscle and flesh and I felt the first needling pleasure at my vital reservoir.

I had a thought to free myself and mount her in the ordinary way. Her limbs leapt voluptuously before my imagination, tits, bum and thighs, all aquiver. But I was unable to move. Gentle, soft, and pneumatic as they were, her nether jaws held my head to its present task with the grip of a vice. My own determination melted along the muscles of my neck. I gave myself up at once to her powerful insistence that I plunge and probe the depths of her hungry pussy, my desiring mouth mining more deeply, like a prospector driven mad by the growing richness and depth of his seam of gold. My hands took a fresh grasp at the putty of her hips, and drew her downward, in a frantic notion, as if drawing her on like a riding boot. The more I strained, blindly and passionately, to be at her body's progenitive fulcrum, the more splendid and seizing was the ringing constellation at my own sex and I was beginning to come, almost against my will, as a huge tide of erotic fire crushed against my inside walls and flushed an urgent jet of jism into the soft mouth that cradled me. At that moment, the bow of my straining body almost reached breaking point. She sucked on my cock as the last drops of jism ejaculated into her mouth and then, at that final moment, her body seemed to decide to join me; she burst apart with pleasure as my tongue continued to probe her pussy parts. Her hips shook wildly. She gyrated and twisted this way and that, and with her hands held my head captive in the jaws of her sex as the last drops of her dew fell upon my tongue. We thrashed about like stranded fish on the soft fur-covered divan and when we came to rest I was still drinking in the lush germinal juices called forth by her body's assertion.

We lay there, momentarily spent. I was stroking the warm wet flesh of her thigh.

She was oiling my belly with a bottle of sweet oil. Her beautiful face with its wet lips and dark, passion-filled eyes was smiling in beatitude. I moved at once, took her in my arms, crushing her startling nipples against my chest, and kissed her on her soft mouth. The taste of our sex juices mingled on our palates. We explored, lipping, tonguing, sucking each other in, unconscious of all else, sealed at our lips and at the sliding meeting of our oiled bellies, dedicated to our prolonged sexual union.

"I want to give you something very special tonight," I whispered. "Now," Nadya whispered. "Now, darling…"

She lay back on the divan, and spread herself open, expecting me to plunge my prick deep into the recess of cunt flesh I'd just had my face buried in for so many delirious moments. But I was intent on conquering yet another dark, tight hole of the wildly sexy Nadya.

"Turn around," I ordered softly, taking the oil from her hands. She flipped over on her belly, and instinctively hoisted her ass up in the air.

I bent down over the bottom globes and delightfully spread them at the cheeks and was met by the stare of the beautifully tight, dark bung hole, with crinkles the color of her nipples, and a firm pucker that I knew would strangle my cock with pleasure.

Not all women like anal sex, mostly because men are too rough and insensitive. But it was my intention that Nadya would scream with pleasure and gush with come when I put myself into her tight little orifice, so first, I prepared her by bending down over the ass crack, running a tongue up and down the length of it, and poking my tongue into the crinkled rim, wetting it, expanding it, opening it with my wet mouth.

She pressed herself onto my tongue; she wanted more.

I started to eat her ass, to gnaw my way into the anal canal softly with teeth and tongue and lips and held her open with two fingers on either side, which prevented her sphincter from instinctively closing around me.

I pulled her closer by grabbing onto the flesh of her ass and hips, and pulled her all the way onto my tongue until it was buried to the very hilt in her ass. And I knew that the feel of closing in, the tightness and the being sucked in that I felt, was on her end a pure, expansive, pleasure, whereupon her ass was being spread and filled simultaneously.

I moved fast, tongue fucking her hole now, and I could see her own hand moving down to her swollen dark clit bud.

"I wish there were a woman here now who could suck me from the other side," she moaned, beginning to masturbate her clit furiously. "Ah, if only Helen Seferis were here to take my cunt into her mouth and lick me, suck me, make my juice come down between her beautiful soft pink lips.

The thought of this, and the very sound of it, made my cock a steel pole that had to find its place inside the tight and tightening orifice of Nadya's asshole. Disengaging my tongue from her bung, I took the oil and began to rub it all over her butt, massaging it generously, and working my way to the crack of her ass with my hands.

I took the side of my hand and slid it down the crack; it was wet, very wet, from the tongue bath I'd given it, but I wanted to make sure she was well oiled for my machine. I worked the oil into her crack, and rubbed it on the dark crinkled rim of her ass, then fingered her, just to work the oil in deep enough.

She moaned: "If Helen were here, she could bury her beautiful face in my cunt and eat me while you fuck me from behind," Nadya was saying, her voice cracked with excited passion. "She'd spread my cunt wide open, and she'd tongue fuck my hole, and then lick my clit, and stroke it with her tongue, until I welled up with pleasure so intense I'd burst.

"And then," Nadya continued, "She'd lick your asshole while you were fucking mine, and she'd find a big, fat, black dildo to stick in your butt while you stuck your big fat cock in mine. And when you were done, she'd take your cock into her mouth and suck you, lick the soil from you, and make you hard again, so she could sit on you and impale those beautiful pink cunt lips on your hard, swollen pole."

I was delirious with passion, and my knob was a massive, swollen piece of meat, that I directed right to the crinkled orifice of Nadya's asshole. It was well oiled, and ready for my rod, and I could feel her shiver with anticipation as I pressed the head to the entrance to the anal canal.

"That's right, fuck my asshole," the tomcat cried,

"and I'll just work my pussy with my fingers, pretending it's Helen's mouth sucking me."

With that, I pressed forward and entered her about an inch. She was wriggling now, not quite yet comfortable with the intrusion of my cock, but hungry to have it deeper, all the way in and past the point of no return.

"Fuck me with every inch of it," she was moaning, "fuck me, please, with all of it, bury yourself. Don't go slow. Rip me open. I want it."

With that, I began to move with greater speed and within moments I was buried in Nadya's tight, sucking asshole to the balls and as I began to pull myself in and out, she began to rub her clit frantically, and was saying, all the while, "Yes Helen, lick me there, lick me like you always do."

The thought of the beautiful, mysterious, blond Helen sucking Nadya's honey cunt while my cock pummeled the black crinkle hole excited me immensely and the combination of Nadya's sensuous movements, her delirious ramblings and the plain old sucking pressure of that tight orifice pulling my cock deeply into its center, had me in the grip of pleasure so profound that I knew I was near exploding.

"How's my little pussy doing," I whispered in her ear, panting. "Is Helen going to make you come while I fuck your asshole, or do you need a helping hand from me."

"Oh yes, put your hand right here," she said, placing it on top of her own, vibrating, frantically frigging fingers. "The come is so close to the edge."

My hand atop hers, we rubbed together on her clit and pretended in our fantasy that the pearly pink lips of the missing Helen Seferis were parted and wrapped around the darkly engorged clit button and as Nadya pressed her butt further up upon my pole I felt myself reach the point of my own no-return, with the come explosion beginning in my lower belly and spreading like a pleasure fire across my thighs and groin.

Simultaneously, Nadya's cunt began to unleash a wild jism explosion. Her hand was rubbing, mine was helping, and the fantasy that she was concocting had her pouring the copious fluids into the mouth of the awaiting blond.

I pressed my plug into her back door outlet one more time as the last of my seed seeped into her oil-filled behind. And she pressed my hand against her pussy as the final spasms shook through her; her anus, at that moment, grabbed at my cock like a clenched fist and seemed to get a stranglehold on me that ensured the very last drops of pearly come juice would be unloaded in Nadya's back door hatch.

We were both exhausted by our wild, animal love making, and the fantasy of Helen Seferis. I fell asleep that night with the beautiful blond, missing pussy on my mind!

Chapter 4

The wheels of the plane left the ground of the Paris airport. Nadya, to whom I had said my goodbyes in the bar before I took off, was presumably on the way to her Paris hotel. She was in the past now, as Laura was, and as were Grisskillin and his mature married ladies.

It had been most difficult with Laura. She called me a fool, and my prospective investigation a wild goose chase. When she saw I was adamant, she became resigned. She sat down, made a number of notes and said that we should require a copy of Helen Seferis' diary for the files. She insisted on this last point. Fortunately, Nadya had a spare copy.

I suppose it was a mistake to take Nadya along to the office, but that morning we had only time to pack my bags at my place, drive to her hotel, drive to the office, and catch the plane.

Laura didn't like Nadya, which wasn't surprising.

As we left, my telling her to get in touch with Grisskillin and tell him that I had left with my charge to Paris, she kissed me on the cheek and told me to look after myself.

In the taxi, Nadya told me that she didn't like Laura. She thought her impertinent. "She's only a secretary, after all," Nadya said. But she soon forgot to be jealous of Laura. As soon as we left London she began to talk about Helen Seferis. Evidently, she felt that her own friend was far more serious competition than my secretary.

"I'm really a fool to send you," she said in a sad voice, and I thought for a moment that she was going to suggest I give up the idea and that we have a honeymoon in Paris. To tell the truth, had she done so, I should probably have consented. However, she did not. Instead she lapsed into silence, a silence which was unbroken almost until we touched down in Paris.

There was no privacy in the bar. We looked at one another. Our imminent parting set a distance between us. We lingered over one drink, saying little or nothing, until the voice came over the loudspeaker to say that the passengers in my plane should make their way to the control room. I put my arms round her and drew her to me. We kissed passionately, oblivious to the other travellers who were swarming about us.

"Come back," she whispered, but I felt even at the time that she didn't believe it.

Some things are impossible. That we should be together always, marry perhaps, was—and I believe we both realized it from the beginning—one of them.

But that didn't lessen the wrench of our actual parting. As I walked away from her, I had the sudden impression that I was mad, stark raving mad. What a fool I was to leave such a perfect creature! But the thought, did not stop my legs from walking, from carrying me right out of her sight. I was frozen, unable to look back, because something told me that if I did so, she would run from where she stood and be safe in my arms again, and then it would be too late to back out, for we should have embarked on our mad venture towards the impossible.

Why impossible? God knows. Perhaps two people with such a violent passion for one another can only destroy themselves by surrendering in a sentimental way. We should have burned one another to death. Had I not had the experience before, with Laura?

Perhaps that was what made me walk without looking back through the control room and out on to the runway. The silver monster was already preparing to taxi off into the takeoff position. I was the last passenger aboard. Only after the doors had slammed and I was seated with my safety belt across my knees did I venture a glance back towards the airport buildings. It was too late now anyway. But she was not there. She must already have taken a taxi to the centre of Paris.

I closed my eyes as the plane began to move forward.

After Nice, as we hovered out above the Mediterranean, my mind slipped naturally into the new situation.

I was on a job. And I did not delude myself for a moment that it was going to be easy. Too much time and too many people had been involved already. An important man had been assassinated. In the Arab world, such an event leaves bad blood. I, by becoming Nadya's agent, had become the agent of that side which had arranged for the murder of an important

Sheikh. Once beyond police protection, I would be in danger of my life.

I settled back comfortably in my seat.

The thought was exhilarating. It served to blow away the cobwebs of my recent romance. Nadya's love, if it really ever existed, was irrelevant. If I made a mistake, she could not save me any more than Pamandari was able to save Helen Seferis. The habit of concentration, the habit of gathering my courage to a small knot in my solar plexus—a habit learnt and ingrained during the war when I moved in and out of Nazi Germany in the shadow of the Gestapo—dissolved the past as hot water dissolves sugar. I felt my cheeks burning, as though I had swallowed a large glass of hard liquor. I no longer missed Nadya, or Laura, or the others. Even Helen Seferis was no more than the climax, if successful, of a mission.

I wondered casually how many mouths I was going to have to break, how many bodies I was going to have to leave behind, dead, or merely seduced, before I got to the root of the problem and brought Helen Seferis back alive to Europe. I wondered whether I had grown soft in the years between the end of the war and now, after half a dozen years in my London practice. My practice, as I have already indicated, seldom moved beyond the world of unfaithful spouses. It was over six years, I suddenly realized, since I had been forced to shoot a man. Tomorrow, it might be different.

Once again the sense of danger passed through me like a shot of whiskey, and when I looked up it was to watch the pleasant balance of the stewardess's buttocks as they moved purposefully away from me between the two rows of seats.

The sight and my reaction to it brought it home to me at last that I was cured.

In many ways, I felt as if I were on a James Bond adventure. Instinctively, I sensed—and hoped for—success and that feeling was more overpowering than the secret fear that I would fail, or even get hurt, on my search for the elusive, the lovely, and the very mysteriously missing Helen Seferis.

I lay my head back in my plane seat and must have dozed, for I drifted into a lovely fantasy dream that starred myself and the pretty black stewardess whose buttocks had caught my attention.

She came up to me in the aisle; her shirt was open, exposing huge, brown breasts with big, cookie-sized dark nipples. She pressed her titties into my face. "Coffee, tea or mother's milk," she said, pressing a huge tit near my lips. "I'll take the latter," I responded, eagerly taking the large, fleshy mammary in my hand and bringing the nipple bud to my mouth. I took it to my lips making loud, sucking noises as I played with the flesh.

"Ever had a black pussy," she asked, maneuvering herself over me in my seat, and then getting herself settled in the seat next to me. "Ever fuck black cunt?"

I felt my prick stiffen at the thought of it because I never had and in that moment, I very much wanted it to be my next adventure.

"Not until now," I said, lifting the armrest between our seats and placing a hand on the long, chocolate thigh.

She wore silky black stockings, held up by a black silk garter, and her pussy and butt were naked beneath her skirt—she'd removed her panties before coming to me in my seat.

The legs were thick and toned, and her ass was high and smooth and big; the flesh was firm and tight and had a milky quality to it.

"Go down on me," she instructed. "Let me spread my black legs for you so you can eat me out. Put your white face between these thighs and eat!"

I felt like we were the only two people on the plane as I maneuvered my head between her legs. She hoisted her skirt, exposing a fine bush of curly, kinky hairs that covered and hid exquisitely—and surprisingly—dark pink cunt lips. They were fat, and contained fold after fold of cunt flesh. The chocolate outer lips and the dark pink inner folds hid the pink opening to her cunthole. I quickly scoured it out and exposed the silky opening—it was wet with anticipation, and the brighter pink inner sanctum called out for my tongue to lick it and my lips to kiss it.

I put my head between her thighs, she spread herself wide open, while leaning back into the third seat in our row, propped up on her elbows.

Her clit was a combination chocolate and pink, and it was huge, like a small, engorged penis. I took it between my lips and gently gnawed it, pressed it together and sucked at it. She moaned with delight.

My cock was rampant, ready to fuck and her cunt was a wet, juicy hole just waiting to be filled.

All the armrests were lifted from between the seats now, and the stewardess laid back, her skirt up to her waist, her stockings still clinging to her ample thigh, her head near the window seat as she spread those thighs as far apart as she could in a plane seat.

"Come on, Mr. Bond," she was cooing, "give me some meat, right here." She had a hand on her cunt, opening the fleshy lips so that her hole was exposed and ready.

I took my cock out of the constraints of my trousers, got over her, and pressed myself to the edge of her opening; she foisted her hips upward.

"Fuck me real good," she begged, "that nice big

cock of yours is as big as any; let me have it all, all of it, now."

In that moment, with the head of my cock kissing the opening to her cunt, I seemed to have lost all control, all semblance of manners, and I simply plowed into the juicy folds of her awaiting slit, and pummeled her, probed her, fucked her to the hilt without so much as a polite pause or slow start.

Her hips were pushing hard against mine and she was hungry to greet them; she wanted to get fucked wildly, and quickly, and she wanted to come. She put her hand between her legs, and between her cunt and my groin, and began to rub that huge clit button of hers as I fucked her and she was soon moaning—moaning right in the middle of an inflight airplane—with wild, passionate, animal like noises.

My cock was being sucked deeply into the fleshy, succulent pussy hole and the base of my cock was surrounded by the meat flesh of her own sex. I felt deliciously smothered and sucked at; I was comfortably being coaxed toward a come as the stewardess continued to meet my thrusts by pressing hard against me, slapping her groin against mine.

I started to fuck wildly, passionately, pounding myself into her like animals pound themselves into other animals, as the two of us simply reacted to base sexual needs and fucked without even introducing ourselves.

"Come on, baby," she was saying, "give it to me, give me some of that white love juice. Pour it in me, pour it in my hole, because I'm going to cream all over your cock in just a second."

With that, she pressed herself onto me and smashed her fat clit against my groin, rubbing, rubbing, rubbing herself into a come frenzy and squeezing the muscles of her cunt as she did.

I started to come as well, pulled into the stranglehold of her snatch, and sucked into the depths of her womb by her twitching pussy as she gyrated her hips against mine.

"Suck my titties," she pleaded, "suck them, now."

With that, I took the huge, chocolate nipples into my mouth, one by one, and sucked eagerly on their tips, just as I felt my own semen exploding into her cunt and felt her juices rushing onto my cock in a creamy combination of emissions. One last cunt squeeze pulled out every drop of my jism.

I fell upon her heaving breasts, we both sighed and relaxed for a moment, then she got up, pulled her skirt over her ample ass, and bent over my cock and licked it clean of all the come juices we'd both brought forth.

Then she stood up, and straightened herself. Then, suddenly, she seemed to be looking over me quite seriously, her uniform back in tact, her blouse all buttoned up with her regulation bow tie neatly tied. Her skirt was no longer rumpled and wrinkled.

She was beside me. "Can I get you anything," she asked as if she were just a stranger passing in the aisle. "We're about to land, better buckle up."

It took me a moment to realize that my fantasy spilled into reality because just after I dreamed the black stewardess was gleefully licking the come from my cock, she was, in reality, standing next to me, asking if I needed anything.

How ironic life sometimes is. I shot her a devious glance, and said, "thank you, I'm fine." She smiled and walked away, and I watched those full, tight twin globes heaving beneath the uniform as she walked toward the front of the plane.

In Algiers, I made my way immediately to a smart hotel. After shaving and bathing, I tried to reach the

Chief of Police by telephone. I was told that he was out of town but that I could see his assistant, Mr. Borthese. I managed to make an appointment for two hours ahead, the same day. He would grant me a short interview at 6 P.M. The time by my watch was 4:30 P.M. I unpacked. I placed the small leather case which contained my 'artillery' in the top drawer of the dressing table and locked it. As yet, I felt no need of being armed. My business in Algiers was merely routine. The police could provide me with the general picture. Later on, I intended to have the official story from one of the government agents at Ghardaia.

I am not a romantic. In my service with the British government I have visited many strange places, places whose very names possess, for the Westerner, an aura of mystery. The first thing that was brought home to me was that these places, these names, do not possess mystery for the native. They are as common, as uninspiring, as natural, as logical as Edgeware Road or Soho. This was brought home to me one night in Istanbul. I was lured by a young Turkish girl into an alleyway. She tensed me into a frenzy, kissing my lips, sucking my tongue, sticking her tongue into my ear and whispering that she was going to get down on her knees, pull my prick out of my pants, and suck my rod until it spilled wildly into her mouth. She rubbed her firm little tits against me and pressed her pussy flesh on my swollen groin. I could have fucked her right there but my thoughts of crescent moons, of the feel and odor of smooth young skin, were abruptly replaced by the consciousness of an indecently long and indecently sharp dagger which pricked the skin at my Adam's apple. The girl, my romance, had disappeared. Instead, her accomplice wooed me: A gruff voice ordered me to be quiet and a rough hand removed my wallet. A few minutes later, I took my disillusionment back into the lighted thoroughfares.

No, the mystery of the East is a figment of the Western mind. Thus, if a woman disappears in North Africa, she has other things being equal, a far better chance of being traced than if she disappears in America. In North America, there are 209,000,000 people, most of them white. In Algeria, there are less than 8,500,000 people—the population of Scotland—and most of them are people of color. The French authorities in North Africa are 'natives'. They have been there for a long time. They have a very efficient police force which does not need to be careful about its methods. My first question was, therefore: What was all this nonsense about no results?

I went down to the bar in a reflective mood, downed a double Scotch and asked for a telephone directory. I found the number I was looking for, and, a moment later, was talking to Freddie Hoyle, an old acquaintance of mine, and a foreign correspondent for several British dailies.

"Look, Freddie," I said when the formalities of greeting were over, "can you meet me in a quarter of an hour? I want some information."

"Sure thing," he said. "There's nothing doing at the moment. I'll be right over."

I thanked him and hung up.

At the bar I ordered another double Scotch, swallowed it, ordered the same again and took myself off to an armchair to wait for Freddie.

In twelve minutes flat he was sitting beside me.

"What brings you?" he said. "Fed up with your dental practice?"

"Yes," I replied. "I was struck off the register for using the wrong drill. I'm, over here to join the Foreign Legion."

I don't know why it is that every time one talks to a newspaper correspondent one must adopt their speech habits, and sense of humor. Here anyway was Freddie, who spoke little else than his own particular brand of journalese, obviously set to bite off a dozen witticisms before he ordered a second drink. I interrupted him before he could get started.

"Listen, Freddie," I said, "I have an appointment at six so I haven't much time..."

"You just arrived!" Freddie protested.

"I'll meet you later," I said, "but for the moment I want you to tell me what you know about the disappearance of a woman called Helen Seferis."

Freddie looked blank, and then, in his own inimitable English, he said: "Look, let's spin the compass and see where we're at."

It was my turn to look blank.

"I mean pass me the ball," he said with a grin.

"The man who kidnapped her was assassinated. He was some sort of Sheikh..." I said.

"Aha! Now I'm with the convoy!" Freddie said with a laugh. He leaned forward as though he were afraid of being overheard. "I did a bit of fishing myself in connection with this. As a matter of fact, two of us did, Mason of The Bugle and myself. We got together on it and decided to up periscope and look around. No soap. Somebody definitely gummed up the works on us."

"Go on."

"Well, you know that Lees and Higginson had their agents over here?"

"I didn't know which firm it was but I knew that there were enquiry agents at work."

"That's the name for them," he said, "Jeezus! They might have been O.K. in the days of Sherlock Holmes! An old-fashioned firm, you understand? No good at all on a job like this. Missing relative and all that. Discreet advertisements in the 'Personal Column'! Well, to cut a long story short, the point was that neither Mason nor I could actually jump into the pond ourselves, I mean we've both got jobs to do, so we had to count on their agent, a guy called Linklater, for our information. He left just last week. Whoever it was hired them called off the dogs."

"Pamandari of Bombay," I said.

"You don't say!"

"Yes, but go on. I want you to tell me what you know."

"Well, Linklater said just before he left that he felt the authorities at Ghardaia weren't so interested in the case as they pretended to be."

"That's interesting."

"Yeah, some colonel called Jerome Poilu. He was in charge of the case."

"What about him?"

"Well, he's been seen a lot lately in the company of the old Sheikh's sister, the one that got bumped, I mean. The new Sheikh is the old one's brother, a guy called Hussein."

I ordered another round of drinks.

"The sister looks like the Queen of Sheba," said Freddie poetically.

"Pro-French?"

"Yes," Freddie said. "There was some talk that the Arab League was mixed up in the assassination of his brother."

"Look, Freddie, all this is very interesting, but I don't see where it gets us. I don't think this has anything to do with politics. The murder of the Sheikh, perhaps; Helen Seferis, no. The dead man kidnapped her. He put her in a brothel. We may assume that his relatives wish to keep her there for sentimental reasons, although I don't see why. Anyway, they are either hiding her from the police or they don't know where she is. Colonel Poilu may very well want to lay the Queen of Sheba, who wouldn't? If she didn't want the girl to be found, he might certainly have gone slow on the investigations. But it seems to me we should start with the Arab, the one who 'found' the document, I mean. Where did he get it?"

"You're asking me," Freddie said.

"What do you know about him?"

"Linklater said he was some kind of pimp. He spoke to him, you know, in that kind of commanding, older statesman voice that few criminals would take seriously, saying things like: 'See here, my good man, where did you get hold of this manuscript?'"

We both laughed.

"They let Linklater interview him in the can," Freddie continued. "Of course it was no dice. The guy wouldn't talk."

"Why didn't the police make him talk?"

"Colonel Poilu," Freddie said with a benign smile.

"That makes sense," I said. "So we might assume for the moment that the Queen of Sheba is interested enough in the Seferis woman not to want the police to beat the information out of the pimp."

"Sure, just like I said."

"Next question: Where is the pimp? Have they sprung him?"

Freddie shook his head. "Search me," he said.

"Can you find out?"

I admit that I had an ulterior motive in asking this question. I could obtain the information myself quite easily from the police. But at the moment I wanted to be rid of poor Freddie, because I had only three-quarters of an hour left before my appointment and a second before I had caught a glimpse of the lonely blonde in the green cocktail dress who was sitting at the bar. She had the nicest pair of ankles I had seen for at least an hour.

"I suppose so," Freddie said.

"Be a good guy," I said, "run along now and find out where I can locate him. If I'm out when you get back, you can leave a message for me."

"You're the boss," Freddie said. "I'll get the dope for you but I doubt if you'll be able to get the guy to talk."

"He'll talk," I said sweetly, "if I have to build a fire under him."

A moment later, Freddie left to get the information for me. As soon as he had gone, I gave one of my cards to the waiter with instructions to give it to the blonde at the bar. He bowed and left.

When she turned round to look in my direction, I got up at once and walked across to her.

I have never believed in allowing business to interfere with pleasure, and this tall girl with her straight blonde shoulder-length hair which shone in the bar lights like some alloy of mercury, her movements slow and indolent in the heat of the African evening, seemed bored and ready as I was for a chance meeting. And anyway, until the time of my appointment there was nothing further I could do. My course of action was quite clear: to derive what information I could from the police in Algiers, to interview the amorous Colonel Poilu, and to make the little pimp understand that the time had come for him to begin talking. To make further plans without further information would have been unscientific, and, under the circumstances—for this interesting young lady was by no means hostile in aspect, looked even more languorous and shapely to closer inspection—unartistic.

"How kind of you to allow me to join you," I said with a small bow.

"I didn't say a word, Mr…?" and she glanced with a smile at the card in her hand. Her voice was husky with a slight trace of a Southern American accent.

"Harvest," I said helpfully. "Forgive me, I interpreted no word as assent."

She laughed. There was a subtle tremor in her voice. "Well, I don't suppose I object exactly…"—she was all the time looking me over—"Because it's a relief to hear someone else speak English."

I sat on the bar stool next to her.

"My friend had to go off," I said. "I was hoping you'd dine with me."

"My name is Rosemary Dalton," she said in an amused voice, "and I'm not sure that I know you well enough to accept your invitation."

"You'll have to make a snap decision, I'm afraid, for I have an appointment at six." I looked at my watch. "I can give you ten minutes. If you say yes, you can come along for the ride."

"In that case, I'll tell you in nine minutes," she said with a bewitching smile.

I inclined my head in polite assent.

"Tell me, Miss Dalton," I said, "what brings you to Africa?"

"African nights," she replied at once. "I always dreamed about them."

"You're like a friend of mine," I said. "A woman called Helen Seferis."

The picture of the unknown woman sleeping on sheepskins in the middle of the desert, waiting for a strange male to visit her, had prompted my remark.

"Tell me about her," Miss Dalton said.

"Ah," I said, "that would take at least during dinner and perhaps half the night as well! She was abducted. She has since been sold to a house of ill repute."

"How fortunate for her," said Miss Dalton drily.

"You think so?"

"How like a man to ask such a question!"

"No, really," I protested, I wanted information, so I was dropping in prompts to see how she'd respond. "You see, according to Helen Seferis, she became aware that that was what she always wanted, to become, as she put it, an object of lust."

My remark appeared to embarrass her. She flushed, a soft suffusion of color under her tan.

"How do you know all this?" she said at last.

"We have her diary," I said. "It goes up to the point at which she is actually in the brothel."

"And then?"

"And then nothing," I replied. "No one knows where she is. That's why I'm here."

"You're here to find her?"

I nodded and reached forward for the whiskey that the barman had pushed towards me.

"But if that was what she wanted...?"

I grinned.

"She's not my employer," I said.

"And you'll find her?"

"Of course, that's what I'm here for."

Miss Dalton laughed.

"Why are you telling me all this?"

"I'm making the most of my nine minutes," I said. "What could be more interesting? If I had talked about the weather you wouldn't be coming to dinner with me."

"What makes you think I will!"

I finished my whiskey.

"Let me help you on with your wrap," I said.

She made no effort to resist as I placed the grey

linen jacket around her shoulders and a moment later she had slipped off the bar stool and was standing beside me. She was about five foot five inches tall, slim, and cool.

"We'll take a taxi," I said.

"No need," she replied. "I have my car outside."

We hardly spoke as she drove me smoothly across the city in the maroon Cadillac convertible. She dropped me at the Prefecture of Police.

"I'll stay in the car," she said. "Don't be too long or I'll drive out of your life."

"You look as though you've driven far enough already," I said, making my way towards the large doors.

I had to wait for a couple of minutes in a front room. Then a fascinating young secretary with jet black hair and buttocks which appeared to have been built into her dress appeared and said:

"Will you come this way, please?"

I followed her at an appreciative distance, my eyes glanced softly in the direction of the compact rhythm of her backside, until, going through another door, and still fascinated by the delicate interaction of the harness and what it harnessed, a man's voice said to me, rather drily, I felt:

"You were looking for something, my dear sir?"

I looked into the eyes of a handsome man of about forty, his hair graying at the temples, immaculately dressed, an expression of bored cynicism on his face. I figured he was the police chief's assistant.

"Merely for information," I said pleasantly. "Mr. Borthese, I presume?"

He ignored my question.

"It is already quite late," he said, standing up and, in the French manner, shaking hands with me.

"Would you be kind enough to tell me what I can do for you?"

"I'm here to find a missing woman," I said, making myself comfortable on one of the leather chairs.

"Ah?" His cynical expression deepened.

"She was last heard of about six months ago."

He shook his head hopelessly.

"This woman was sold to a brothel…" I began.

"Then my dear sir," he interrupted, "please take it from me that your search will prove fruitless. Six months is a long time. Anything might have happened. This is not Europe, you must understand…"

I allowed him to go on. His pretty secretary was sitting at a side desk. I had the distinct impression that he was performing for her. Her eyes were amused beneath demure lashes.

"I realize, of course," he went on affably, "that this must sound shocking to the English sensibility, but I assure you that it is like looking for a needle in a haystack. We will of course," he said, adopting his most official tone, "do our utmost to locate this woman's whereabouts. I suppose some kind of inheritance is involved? Well, we shall certainly do our best. My secretary here will give you a form. It is the standard one for missing persons. You should fill it out, explaining your reasons for believing that she has been—er—passed on to a brothel, etcetera, and then leave it to us. If anyone can find her, we can. But as I said at the beginning, I don't hold out much hope. And now, sir, if you will excuse me, I have an important appointment!"

He made to shake hands with me. I watched his hand settle back to his side with an imperturbable smile.

"You understand, sir," he said in a tone of annoyance, "that I, personally, can be of no further help to you?"

I allowed thirty seconds more silence.

"My name is Harvest," I said pleasantly. "I'm not asking you to find this woman. I am going to do that."

His smile was one of amused contempt. I ignored it.

"You have already had nearly six months to find Helen Seferis," I said.

His expression changed instantly.

"You are looking for Miss Seferis?"

I nodded. "What did you do with the Arab?"

The question, as I had calculated, took him by surprise. He retreated behind his highly polished desk before he answered.

"Gone months ago," he said in a defensive tone. "No evidence. We had to let him go."

"Rubbish."

"Sir?"

"Rubbish," I repeated with a grin. "Who let him go? Colonel Poilu?"

He eyed me dangerously.

"As you are probably aware," he said in an icy tone, "Colonel Poilu was in charge of the case. He is resident in that area, a highly efficient officer, and his judgment on the matter was not questioned by us."

"Evidently not," I said drily. I leaned forward with a smile: "What I'm asking you is why wasn't it questioned?"

"I don't know by whose authority you ask such an impertinent question," my interviewer said slowly. "I assure you…"

"Let me do the assuring," I said roughly. "The White Slave Racket is one of the main fields of Interpol. Mr Pamandari is exceedingly annoyed to find that one of your officers has become an accessory after the fact in this case. I want to warn you now that unless I have your cooperation there is going to be trouble. Every important newspaper in Europe will demand an investigation into your department."

My bluff worked, probably because, whichever way you looked at it, it wasn't all bluff. Grisskillin and Pamandari between them were probably quite capable of arousing the indignation of half the world. I sat back with a patient smile on my face.

My interviewer seemed to be searching for his words.

"Your charge is a serious one," he said hesitantly. "An error of judgment perhaps, but I assure you that Colonel Poilu is incapable of the kind of action which you impute to him. What possible reason could he have?" At this point he laughed with a kind of nervous relief.

"Ask Rirha bent Ali," I said with a small smile.

Mr. Borthese became pale.

As I had leaned over his desk I noticed his name on various bits of correspondence, confirming it was indeed Borthese I was speaking with. "Look here," I continued, pressing home my advantage, "you know the situation as well as I do. Helen Seferis was kidnapped by Sheikh Youssef ben Ali who was assassinated at Laghouat a few months ago. The new sheikh is Hussein ben Ali, his brother. But there is also a sister, Rirha, a beautiful woman, I believe. Colonel Poilu thinks so anyway. Now, although I can't see for the moment why this woman should be interested in destroying Helen Seferis, I can only conclude from Colonel Poilu's strange behavior that she is interested in doing just that. An experienced officer let the key witness go. The diary was found on him. He never explained where he got it. Why didn't Colonel Poilu make him explain?"

"Witnesses can be stubborn," Borthese suggested uneasily. "It's not always so simple to get them to talk."

"You could have held him for much longer than you did as a suspect on a white slavery charge."

"I suggest that you talk to Colonel Poilu himself."

"I shall, as soon as I get to Ghardaia. Meanwhile, I want some other information. Roughly speaking, in what direction do you think they took her?"

"It's difficult to say," he hedged.

"It's not difficult to say," I snapped. "She was taken by caravan for weeks across desert! They went south obviously, roughly speaking towards Tamanrasset, Touareg country."

"Mr. Harvest," the police official said politely, "it is quite obvious that you know as much about it as we do in Algiers. I suggest that the only person who can give you further information is Colonel Poilu himself."

I got up. Obviously Mr. Borthese had decided not to be cooperative. I told him I wished a file with photographs of the Arab on whom the manuscript of the diary had been found. He said icily that his secretary would obtain it for me. I bid him good-day. There was nothing further to be done. At least I had corroborated my original suspicion that the police had not done everything they could have in the matter. I had also, by the way, and I regretted it to some extent, set them against me. Borthese would probably get in touch with Poilu immediately and tell him I was on my way. Well, it couldn't be helped. I at least knew from what quarter I could not expect help. I took the file the pretty secretary brought me, overcame an urge to make a pass at her, and went downstairs towards the street. I wondered if the handsome Mr. Borthese was boffing the pretty nymph, if she would walk back into his office, pull his dark skinned shaft from his uniform and press her mouth upon his cock, offering a brief respite from the stressful feelings I'd left him with. Would he then bid her to part her silky thighs, show him her black pussy fuzz, and let him put his rampant rod deep into the crevice of her cute little cunt?

I imagined it to be a tight, juicy, pink little slit, with fluffs of dark hair covering both the muff and sides of the cunt lips.

It was the kind of cunt, I bet, that could make a man cream quickly and efficiently, because of its tightness and youth. My cock was so hard after standing up to the unhelpful police official that I could have poked her right there, I could have tossed her onto Borthese' desk, right in front of him, and pressed my own huge weapon home into the cunt of his cute little secretary.

Thinking of that pink, wet slash of girlhood between her legs gave me a huge erection, and I wanted to put it somewhere. The fire of desire, spurred on by the feeling that I was at least getting someplace with my investigation, burned in the vicinity of my underwear. Luckily I had just the cure waiting outside for me in the car.

The Cadillac was still there.

"I was just about to drive away," Miss Dalton said sweetly as I climbed in.

We drove smoothly through the crush and welter of Algiers, out of the main boulevards where European dress was predominant, up the hill past the bazaar or market where crates of oranges and poultry were stacked and an occasional ancient truck spurted its tinny noise and dust amongst the peddlers of dates, almonds, worthless jewelry, leather goods and citrus fruits. An occasional mangy dog leapt away from under the tentative forward movement of our front wheels. A skinny beggar with one sightless porcelain eye thrust his arm through the window of the car. It was like a crooked broomstick on which the hand hung heavily like a large leather gauntlet.

"*Anna meskine*! *Anna meskine*!" the voice croaked at us from the other side of the glass.

I dropped some coins into the palm and the thin grayish arm retreated. As we moved on, the face tilted questioningly behind us and the goat's-beard glinted in the sun. My last glimpse was of the scrawny throat, a light coffee color, the Adam's apple prominent in profile.

"The restaurant is not far," I said. "Take the next turn on the right."

We bumped along a narrow dirt road towards a square in the center of which there was a fountain. Around the fountain several cars with foreign and local number plates were already parked. A black man in a red fez gave us parking directions. We climbed out of the car and strolled over to the restaurant. It was called Le Bosphore.

At the other side of the bead curtains we encountered Ahmed, the Turkish proprietor, whom I had met once during the war. He gave us an enthusiastic welcome and ushered us to one of the low brass tables. Similar tables, some of them already occupied, were grouped round a central floor where the clients, if they wished, could dance. It was also the locale of one of the most sensual cabarets in North Africa.

"You are a little early, Mr. Harvest," Ahmed muttered apologetically. "The girls do not arrive for another half an hour. Meanwhile, an aperitif?" I nodded, helping Rosemary with her seat.

She was fascinated by the exotic decor. The ceiling was low, the woodwork intricately carved and studded with mother-of-pearl. The atmosphere was hung heav-

103

ily with some exotic perfume. A naked cigarette girl stood like a statue against a bead curtain, the lights flitting soft shadows across the sheer pale surfaces of her flesh, and glinting at the strong haired thrust of her mound. The clients, for the most part, ignored her, occasionally, indolently, casting pale disinterested eyes in her direction. She met their glances without expression. She might indeed have been a statue.

"She looks strong," Rosemary whispered huskily. There was a slight tremor in her voice. I concluded I had not made a mistake. Like many women of her class, that is to say, women with looks and money, women who can go where they went when they want, she was the victim of an almost tragic sexual longing. Sexual, because it involved the heat and satisfaction of her body. Tragic, because this desire was seldom specific. It was difficult for her to locate the object of her desire, understandably, because it was rather a state of herself which she fought to make articulate. It was as though she longed to become involved in a vast impersonal sexual nightmare, and this strong cool Arab girl with her solid opaque flesh fired her imagination. Here was nakedness, slick, taut, unquestioned. The breasts were infinitely suggestive, not so much because of their young elasticity or the mass, but because of the long pale pink nipples, each as long almost as the butt of a cigarette. Almost obscene, but irresistibly erotic. She was flesh, flesh which had been experienced, loved, doted upon, flesh which had been used and would surely be used again.

I knew, in Rosemary, there was a desire to be with the same sex, to go to the strong Arab girl, take the emotionless face between her hands, draw the dark lips to her own, and kiss her with the wild abandon she may even be too afraid to bestow upon a man.

The vision of Rosemary kissing the girl excited my sex organ, roused me into an erection, and made me long to see the cool, sophisticated blonde approach the Arab and take those long, obscene nipples between her tender, proper mouth and suck them like a baby sucking milk from a mother's breast.

Then she could take the cigarettes from the girl, lay them on the floor, and lay the naked girl down on a table; the same table, perhaps, we were to dine on. Yes, I could watch the oppressed, explosive blonde hungrily open the dark, lean, long thighs of the naked girl and kiss her way down from the mouth, to the titties, to the belly.

She'd plant smooth, short, lovingly gentle kisses on the flat stomach as the girl, beginning to respond, would press her hips upward into the air as she felt her own cunt lips begin to swell with the pleasure caused by the seductive blonde. Rosemary would work her way down, daintily, to the lips that poked their fat, juicy folds from beneath the dark cunt fur, and would lick, softly, silently, up and down the length of the cunt.

The Arab girl, now passionate, would pull Rosemary to her by the blond head of hair, and press the face down closer to her swollen cunt as she moaned and groaned in pleasure.

This is where I could step in and assist my new blond friend. I'd softly bend to kiss and suck the incredible titties of the Arab girl as Rosemary proceeded to gamahuche the girl's quim. Although it is her first jab at burying that pretty face into another woman's cunt, she is lavishly, expertly eating pussy as if it's an innate talent.

I am meanwhile playing with the breast, squeezing the nipples between my fingers and pressing the titties close to one another, sucking both long nipples at once. The pleasure of this is shooting into the dark-skinned girl's slit and the juicy emissions of her sexual joy are beginning to well in her belly, and the fire is spreading throughout her cunt, up and down her groin and thighs, through her asshole.

She is moaning loudly now, chanting in her native tongue, and I bend over the now-expressive mouth and kiss her with rapt attention, my tongue exploring the depths of her pink upper lips, and the beautiful blonde's tongue probes the deepest recesses of her lower lips and sucks on the dark, lovely clit bud, bringing the girl to a high pitch of cunt-fire excitement.

I hold her chin in my hand as I kiss her, experiencing the richness of her passion as she heaves and sighs into my mouth. One hand caresses the titties, the nipples now hard and big and swollen, like small pieces of wood. Rosemary is lapping her cunt up now, and all I can see is the blond head moving up and down, all around, as if devouring the dark-lipped cunt in front of her. She's wild with passion, and the Arab girl, so close to coming, is kicking her legs, pushing her cunt into Rosemary's face, chanting noisily, that she is about to explode from within the very depths of her soul.

I intuitively go back down to suck the titties and I can feel in the heaving breast that the cunt below is about to explode into the mouth of the first-time cunt licker, and the Arab girl holds Rosemary's face so tight to her clit that Rosemary can barely breathe, but she doesn't even care, as she licks and sucks the girl off into the ultimate, tabletop, pussy explosion. She holds the thrashing legs down toward the end, so she can keep the cunt still enough to lick the clit that will bring the final contractions, and then, the creamy emission, onto her mouth. She's holding the girl's thighs so tightly now, because she's writhing so, that Rosemary's fingers are leaving pink impressions on the thighs as she licks up and down the shaft to collect the last of the juices on her tongue.

She rises, and smiles with the satisfaction of successfully eating a cunt into a creamy state of come, and, her own pussy on fire, she strips her panties and skirt off right there and climbs upon the table, planting her cunt right onto the Arab girl's waiting lips.

She's so on fire, so hot, that it won't take much to set her off. I can see the Arab girl spread the pink slash apart and lick into the wet, juicy hole between the lips of Rosemary's cunt, and Rosemary shivers with anticipation as the tongue gently darts around to her engorged and swollen clit. The Arab girl takes the hard pink bud between her dark lips and sucks while she spreads the lips of the cunt apart, playing with them, touching the swollen sides of Rosemary's slash, to create a gentle pressure and pleasure in her sex.

I cannot resist. I bring my lips to Rosemary's and put my tongue deep inside the lovely mouth, kissing her, and tasting the natural flavor of the cunt she has so exquisitely licked. She is panting and gyrating her cunt down onto the Arab girl, crazed with the excitement of her wet, swollen cunt.

She is moaning now, into my mouth, as I kiss her, and she puts her arms around my neck, holding me for support as the girl begins a seriously sensuous sucking of Rosemary's cunt lips and clit while expertly inserting fingers into both her swollen cunthole and her twitching asshole, so Rosemary's cunt is now filled with fingers and her ass is filled as well. The mouth of the Arab girl is simply lavishing licks and sucks onto the rest of the severely swollen, hot pink pussy.

"I-I-I'm going to come," she pantingly whispers into my ear. "She's sucking the come right out of m-m-me."

With that she grabs hold of my mouth and presses her tongue so deeply she nearly chokes me, and meanwhile, she's gyrating and pressing her pussy onto the Arab girl's mouth for the final release; I can feel her whole body tense and know the pussy and ass muscles must now be clenching closed and biting down on the fingers that fill them as they press forth into the final stages of orgasmic contractions.

The girl presses her fingers into both holes to the hilt, and then lavishly gives Rosemary's wet, spent pussy a tongue bath to lick up the tidings of her fancy tongue- and finger-work.

Rosemary stays in that position and holds on to me, until I gently lift her up and off the face of the naked cigarette girl, whose chin and cheeks and lips are delightfully wet with Rosemary's juices. I bend down, and lick the side of the girl's cheek, just to taste what I know I will later have possession of myself—Rosemary's cunt.

My cock felt like a rock-hard piece of meat knocking against my trouser zipper, after lapsing into that wonderfully hot vision of Rosemary's first cunt-to-cunt experience. Perhaps, I thought, she might get to experience it for real by the end of the night.

The whole atmosphere, the warm North African night, the mint tea that was brought to us in filigreed glasses, the immensely fat Egyptian who sat between two solemn dark young women, whose kohl eyes were like the eyes of fawns and whose ample thighs under rich silk were alternatively pressed and patted by one of his chubby and obscenely ringed hands—everything was loaded with suggestion.

The Egyptian's eyes were small and pale, with a

slight squint which, for a moment, held Rosemary's eyes, like a snake's or a rabbit's. When he moved his head, it was to bow; respect tinged with insinuation.

I could see that Rosemary was affected. Her cheeks had a high color. The intensely physical implication of everything which surrounded her struck her forcibly.

A small box of gold-tipped cigarettes had been placed in front of us. As I held the match for Rosemary, I was aware of the glance of the Egyptian. His small meaningful eyes bored right into hers. She inhaled deeply, nervously, conscious of the obscene gaze but caressed by it. The hand which held the cigarette, slender, tanned, with beautifully manicured nails, was trembling. I glimpsed her proud profile struck in a pose which was intended to deny the existence of her admirer, but it crumbled and she quivered, her eyes at last drawn back to the squint gaze which lecherously undressed her.

"He wants you," I whispered softly in her ear. She shuddered, but it was almost, though horrified, with pleasure.

A dish of couscous with various piquant sauces was brought to us. The cigarettes, which had, of course, contained a small amount of 'kief' (hashish), were already finished. Rosemary had lost most of her American woman's poise and was like a half open flower. She was unable to keep her eyes away from the Egyptian. Her sleek blonde hair brushed back over her temples had caused a slight perspiration to collect above her high cheekbones. Her superb lips were slightly parted, expectant. Meanwhile, I had caught the eye of one of the doll-like women who accompanied the Egyptian and beneath a veil of inexpression in her dark eyes—they reminded me forcibly of Nadya's—I thought I caught a glimpse of passion.

A belly dancer, naked except for a wisp of silk at her loins, was twitching her navel voluptuously within the oval gleam of her oiled belly. Her movements were accompanied by a kind of flute and Arab fiddle. The place was filling up. A French officer sat with a superb woman in the background, almost hidden. The perfume and the smoke of the exotic cigarettes mingled, making the light-infused atmosphere electric. Nothing moved beyond the belly which did so with slow elastic jerks, and the smoke laden air, impregnated by the wail of flute and fiddle, drifted lazily about it.

Rosemary was fascinated. She did not speak, almost, she seemed to have lost the power to do so. I felt the pressures working inside her. She saw in this moment the possibility of giving articulation to the force, the lust, which disturbed her. Her eyes swung between the oiled navel and the look of insinuation the Egyptian directed on her. I decided to pander to her desire, which, I realized, had an air of intimacy about it and which lived for its satiation.

I called Ahmed and spoke a few words in his ear. Behind his discreet smile, all emotion, all question was hidden.

He said only: "She is sure?"

I smiled. I put my hand on Rosemary's knee. She quivered.

"Ahmed will show you where to go," I said softly in her ear.

She froze momentarily, hesitated, without looking at me, and then, as though her limbs controlled her, she got up and mechanically turned to follow him. I couldn't be sure she knew what she was going for, that is to say, what beyond the amorphous, the unknown, but she knew she was being involved in some vast sexual trauma of her own choosing. And I believe she knew this would be an experience in which she would assert the direction of her own lust. Her body cried out to be involved in the implication of all that subtly and sensuously turned about us, I was quite sure. Her hunger, as I noticed from her breathing, had attained that impersonal, that cosmic dimension beyond personality; it required the immense nature of the unknown in return. Dark blood moved in her and cut at her womb like a blunt stake. She walked gracefully, her immaculate buttocks trembling, like a sleepwalker in the wake of Ahmed towards…herself.

A moment later, I nodded to the gross Egyptian. His little mouth smiled within his fat face. He bowed. He raised his obese body to short, immaculately clad legs and waddled off in the direction they had taken.

I went on looking across the floor, beyond the dancer who still involved herself in a powerful but minute gyration at her navel, at the fragility of the doll-eyes, which, now that they had witnessed the departure of their master, were nakedly lustful. I rose, slipped round the dancer, and raised the warm creature to her feet. She dropped her eyes but allowed herself to be led. I ushered her in front of me through a bead curtain, up one flight of narrow stairs and into a small candle-lit room in the center of which there was a divan. She lowered herself on to it immediately and spread her legs for me.

I found her hot young thighs smeared with the honey of her lust.

At that moment a door closed somewhere below and the noise of flute and fiddle were abruptly cut off from us.

My little belly dancer had no trouble enjoying herself with a man and the sensual little slut made sure the two of us had a fine time during those moments of lust in the upstairs room.

The whole environment was about sex, fucking, lustful abandon of protocol. And Fatima—that was her name—was all about pussy, wide open, waiting pussy; pussy that required no oiling for entry. Her honey-coated cuntway was just ripe for me to enter.

And as much as I love to lick a woman's cunt, or tongue fuck her ass before I plug her, this time, I just went in. My cock head, poised at the entranceway to heaven, got a nice start up when Fatima herself wrapped her strong, lean legs around my butt and pulled me to her.

I kissed her fat, ripe lips, and then slipped my tongue into the warm, wet mouth. I could taste the faint spices of her dinner, and inhaled the sweet scent of her young breath, as my tongue probed the dark, deep wetness of her mouth.

Then suddenly I realized that I was putting my lovely belly dancer to shameful use, fucking her missionary style, for if anyone could wiggle and fuck my brains out from above, it would be her. Keeping her legs wrapped around me, I held her butt and legs and I turned us around. I rolled under her. Now, she was sitting straight up on my pego.

She began to moan as a look of total lust overcame her. You could tell she truly had her fill of me from this vantage point, as my prick pressed up to her womb, filling her to the hilt.

Catching her balance in this new position, she began to slowly move her inner thighs, her butt, and her cunt in a delicious up and down movement, as if dancing while she sat on my cock. Soon, she was tilting most deliciously backward, cunt rubbing up and down against me as my prick moved in and out of her, tantalized by the friction caused by the position.

She was leaning backward even more now, her hands behind her, resting on either side of my knees, and I could see the dark-haired pussy muff move up and down and feel the startlingly tight cunt lips squeeze my organ with each rise, and again, with each fall of her cunt to my cock.

She reached a hand behind her to my balls and began to squeeze them into a pure feeling of ecstasy—lightly, teasingly, gently—as she moved her snatch up and down on my pole.

Soon, she was beginning to shake her bottom and her belly, as if belly dancing on my cock, and my organ, buried deep within her, was receiving the most delicious vibrations as a result of her movements.

Now I could see, as I watched her atop me, the stomach muscles flexing expertly, the hips moving with momentum up and down, and swaying from side to side, and the pussy fur simply lifting up and down, off my cock and back on, at such a delicious pace that I felt my organ turn into a rocket ship about to blast off.

Sensing I was near, she moved her long-nailed fingers to my nipples and lightly, but firmly, squeezed the male bud between the red nails, creating an exotic and different kind of excitement, which shot through my nipples and seemed to travel down to my groin.

I started to come. She felt it, and placed a hand back onto my balls where she delightfully squeezed the two testicles from behind, pressing the orgasmic explosion upward from the source, just at the moment of my coming. It was exquisite, done with impeccable timing.

She rubbed herself downward, as if to sop up any remaining come, and then lifted herself from my shaft, preparing to retreat back to her belly dancing.

She got off the divan, grabbed a warm wet towel from a bowl on the table, and sponged me clean of my own jism.

Then, without a word, she winked at me and was off.

When I returned to the main room, the other dark maiden who had accompanied the Egyptian was gone. Fatima, the girl to whom I had just made love, had also disappeared. I sat down in my old place and smoked a cigarette. It was not long before I realized that the French officer and his mistress were also gone.

I waited for about half an hour, and then I strolled outside and sat in the parked car. I was trying to imagine the scene which would by this time have taken place between Rosemary and the Egyptian. Her white, slim, supple flesh stretched out under his obscene gaze, his pudgy hands exciting her with gentle movements at her breasts and center, to the moment at which his fat body thrust downward on top of her and enjoyed her—the thought of the spectacle almost made me wish that I had not got rid of Fatima so soon. My cock was once again hard, ripe, ready to plunge the depths of a tight, welcoming cunthole.

I imagined that Rosemary perhaps was at this very moment so thoroughly working through her disturbing sexual desires that she would be turned into a heated, horny, unstoppable sexual animal.

And it would all start with the fat Egyptian, who, at that moment perhaps, had Rosemary Dalton bowed between his fat legs, her head bobbing up and down on a huge, fat and imposing penis. I could see the beautiful blond sucking on his organ, not liking the taste or smell of it, liking the man, nor anything about him, but loving the reckless abandon with which she could give of her sexual self and receive within her sexual self.

The fat man probably held her head as she sucked him, so he could control the motion, careful not to come too quickly, for surely he had many games up his sleeve.

I bet his two girlfriends were assisting him; the doll-like girls probably held the legs apart so the fat Egyptian could peer and ogle the gorgeous pink cunt flesh of Rosemary, the cuntflesh I myself longed to bury my face in.

One girl would open the lips, I bet, as he prepared to go down between the legs of the lovely Rosemary Dalton with the technical sexual skill of a master. He'd lick, he'd suck, he'd fondle the pink pussy flesh, until she was so excited, so hot, so ready that he would ram her hole with the huge stiffness of his manhood. Or perhaps, he'd administer the pleasures slowly.

I could see the doll-faced girl with the dark eyes eagerly eyeing the precious cunt petals as her master licked them up and down, and plunged a hungry tongue into the wet, gaping oil slick between Rosemary's legs.

And perhaps, as he did this, he would take one moment out and, with a face filled with Rosemary's cunt juices, he'd kiss the doll-faced girl, tongue her a bit and the two mouths would kiss over Rosemary's pussy; and this would signify that the girl could now participate.

From there, the master and the doll-faced girl would eat the hot wet cunt of Rosemary, who was probably now a twitching, writhing mass of nerve endings, thrilled and awed to have girl lips and the fat Egyptian man's lips lapping at her quim.

I could see those long, lithe thighs shivering and

shaking, as the two simultaneously gamahuched her, the doll-faced girl focusing on her clit, the man, ramming his fat tongue into the pussy hole. The other girl, perhaps, would be toying the her breasts, licking them, sucking the nipples as the cunt experienced the multi-tongue effect.

The fat man would then rise onto his knees between the quivering thighs of my beautiful blond friend and he'd look at the desire in her eyes, the thirst for whatever it was she needed to experience. He'd see her surrender, so complete and so authentic. Clapping his hands, the two girls would sit on either side of Rosemary, splaying her legs wider and wider apart, and the fat Egyptian would poise at the opening to her love portal, the big purple head of his weapon pressed up to the doorway of her sex.

She'd be told not to move, not to budge, to just lie there, receptive, ready to receive whatever he was to offer, and not to try to take more before the time was right.

The two girls, whose own cunts were welling up with sex fire as this went on, would hold Rosemary's legs down, massaging them to keep them still. When they'd felt her responding to the urge to press upward, they pressed her hips back onto the divan.

The fat man's cock would pass the portal, the head lodged right on the other side of the cunt opening. He'd stay there for what, to Rosemary, might seem an eternity, holding himself up on stubby arms as his fat butt and chubby legs floated above her beautiful, milky flesh. I could just see the thick, dark penis pressed an inch or so into the beautiful, pink cunt lips, surrounded by an elegant tuft of blond pussy fur.

He'd press in another inch, and she'd try to greet him, to pull him in more. The girls would hold her

116

down, keep her from doing anything but accepting his thrust, his offering of the moment.

Rosemary's hot cunt muscles would start to twitch around the huge head of his cock, trying to suck him in. He would pull out a little, just to tease, and she would calm the involuntary cunt muscle movements just so he would give her more cock, give it to her just a little deeper.

"This is the true essence of female sexuality," the fat Egyptian would whisper in her ear in broken English. "The pussy is to be filled by a man, as he chooses, and the woman who can accept this, who can be a true receptacle to male lust and movements, is the woman who will have true power over her own sexuality—and power over a man."

With that, he'd bring himself deeper into her cunt, pressing far enough to make her feel the fullness of his eight inches. And her cunt, so wet and swollen now, would again be grasping at his pole involuntarily. But this time, he would let it be and simply push further, deeper into the pussyhole.

His own controlled lust was now to be abandoned and although Rosemary was to remain still, his thrusting would become fast, deeper and finally, all of his eight inches of fat cock was introduced to her love canal and the girls, massaging the tops of her thighs, were simultaneously moving her clit in such a way that it was rubbing deliciously against the dark-haired pubic mound of the fat Egyptian.

And Rosemary, I knew, would be close to coming, close to spilling her milky come onto the fat cock of the Egyptian and in the most delicious way.

"You move now, as I tell you," he'd instruct her, his own huge organ and balls swelled with impending orgasm. "And together we will explode into the North African night."

He would press his cock in to the hilt. "Move slightly, up, yes, to greet me," he'd instruct. He'd press in further, and grab her by the flesh of her hips and ass, pulling the pink cheeks toward him; he'd be capturing the pink, furry cunt between the sandwich of his grasp and his cock.

"Now move ever so slightly, rubbing yourself on me, without pulling away too much," he'd say, holding her firmly in his grasp.

She would feel herself begin to reel with pure delirious pleasure as her cunt filled with cock, her ass flesh pulled toward his hips; the friction of her clit on his groin would bring the come down in a subtle, smooth and deliciously creamy emission.

He would just simply rub it gently out of her and as he felt her cunt ring clasp around his rod as it contracted with the squirting juice of her come, he would release his own juice into the hot portal between the milky legs of Rosemary Dalton.

I could just see the girls so lightly holding her legs down still and the fat Egyptian, pressing her tightly to him in true Arabian fuck-style, as he filled her most disturbing fantasy and made her explode in unbelievable, controlled spasms of come—unlike any other she'd ever known.

And I wished it had been me, administering such a delicious fuck to Rosemary, but I suppose it had to be the fat Egyptian so she could bet the full effect of pleasure, pleasure derived even in a seemingly unpleasurable situation—at the hands of a lecherous foreigner with a fat dick and great sexual prowess.

I suppose I must have spent an hour pondering like this. And then, suddenly, I became alarmed. After all, I was responsible for Rosemary. She was old enough to make her own decisions in regards to her sexual life, but in North Africa one thing leads to another, to force perhaps. I walked quickly past the fountain and entered Le Bosphore for the second time. I went straight to Ahmed's office.

He confronted me with a smile. He anticipated my question.

"Not to be worried, Mr. Harvest!" He came from behind his desk with a knowing smile. "See, I have here two letters for you!'

I took them from him without replying.

The first was a short note from Rosemary. It read as follows:

Dear Anthony,
Don't worry about me. I'm going for a few days somewhere where I'm sure I want to. Hope to see you on your return journey through Algiers.

Many thanks,
Rosemary Dalton

The second was less reassuring. It read:

Dear Mr. Harvest,
It has come to our attention that you are in Algeria for purposes which are not in our interest.
Our advice to you is to leave the country by tomorrow evening: plane 6:15 P.M. from airport.
If you do so, Miss Dalton will be returned to her hotel unharmed. If not, you will never see her again.
This is not an idle threat.

The note was unsigned. I thrust them both into my pocket.

"I want the name and the address of that Egyptian," I said to Ahmed.

"I am afraid that is impossible," Ahmed said with a shrug. "I have never seen him before."

Something told me he was lying. I took a step towards him and found myself looking into the ugly snout of a blunt-nosed automatic.

"You will leave now, Mr. Harvest," Ahmed said gently. "I want no trouble here."

"You've picked the losing side, Ahmed," I said with a grin. "I'm going to make you sorry you were ever born." I said this latter slowly and I caught a flicker of fear in the nightclub proprietor's eyes. I had met him before. He knew me.

But he didn't give way. He spoke gruffly. "I don't intend to get mixed up in this Mr. Harvest. Please go now and if you take my advice you will do as you're told."

I made as if to go, ducked suddenly and hit him just below the knees with my right shoulder. He folded like a jackknife, the gun clattering from his hand across the floor. Before he had time to recover, I lifted a cut glass ashtray from his desk and brought it down heavily on his skull. He groaned and lay still. I walked across the room and pocketed the automatic. Then I selected a bottle of whiskey, poured myself a large shot, and poured the rest over Ahmed's head. As I threw back the whiskey, he looked at me hatefully from the floor.

"I'm going to give you ten seconds, Ahmed, and then I'm going to get to work on you," I said with a grin. "His name and address. You lie to me and I'll kill you."

"You will be sorry..." he began, but a small vicious jab of my foot into his solar plexus silenced him.

"Cut out the crap, Ahmed! You've got five seconds!"

He groaned. He looked as though he was about to retch, but the words came in a kind of desperate whisper: "His card is on the desk...under the blotter..."

Without taking my eyes off him I found the card and put it in my pocket. "Next time," I said, "it would be easier if you talk first." I lifted him by his lapels, gave him one sharp thrust to the belly and, as his head tilted forward, I gave him a sharp rabbit punch to the back of the neck. He crumpled and fell. I stowed him unconscious in a closet, his hands strapped behind him and his mouth stuffed with a handkerchief.

I looked at my watch. It was just midnight. I walked quickly out through the nightclub, stepped into the car and drove slowly past the fountain on the way back to town.

I drove back to my own hotel where I found that Freddie had left a message for me. It read:

Pimp: Abdelkader ben Tahar; seen a couple of weeks ago in Ghardaia, Sun Bar. Colonel Poilu in Algiers today with Rirha bent Ali. Thought it might interest you. When do I see you?

Freddie.

My mind immediately returned to the nightclub where I had caught sight of a French Officer with a superb looking Arab woman. I wondered if they might have been Poilu and his mistress. And the Egyptian, where did he come in? Imagine, I thought he was some sexual master with prowess that would knock the wind out of Rosemary Dalton! His name was Zarouk and the address on the card, the Hotel Excelsior. I asked the desk clerk where the Excelsior was and returned to the car.

Two minutes later I strode through the foyer of the Egyptian's hotel, one of the many deluxe ones in Algiers, and made my way to the residents' bar. My hunch, if it can be called that, was correct. Mr. Zarouk's mountain of flesh straddled one of the

huge armchairs and his dangerous squint was turned
smilingly on the superb woman whom, two hours
before, I had seen in the company of the French
Officer. Poilu was not there. I walked straight across
to their table, arranged a vacant chair and sat down
upon it.

The woman turned her almond-shaped eyes in my
direction. There was a flicker of amusement in her
expression. Her dark hair was brushed flatly against
her temples, and her superb cheekbones gave her
face a scornful look. Zarouk focused his ambiguous
squint upon me. His look betrayed no sign of recog-
nition. They waited for me to speak. I did so only
after lighting a cigarette, inhaling deeply, and blowing a mouthful of smoke into Zarouk's fat face. His
eyes glittered dangerously.

"Where's Miss Dalton?" I said with a smile.

They looked at one another. Rirha laughed softly.
Zarouk smiled at her, but his smile was gone when he
turned to face me again.

"I don't know who you are, sir, and I have never
heard of Miss Dalton. So if you will please leave
now? We wish to be alone."

I didn't budge.

"Where's Poilu?" I said politely.

The Egyptian's eyes narrowed. The woman
watched us with distant interest.

"If you don't go, I shall call the maitre d'hotel and
have you thrown out."

Threats have always been an inspiration to me. I
find it difficult to act unless I have been threatened,
but once a man has threatened me, I find it a pleasure to break his head for it. The head of the
Egyptian was like an overripe melon.

"We're going upstairs to your suite," I said. "We'll
start the search there."

"We go nowhere with you," Zarouk said.

Still smiling, I leaned across the table and slapped his face. The blow rang out like a pistol shot, causing a livid weal to appear on his pale cheek.

Rirha watched like a dangerous cat.

After his first surprise, Zarouk contrived a smile.

"It will be a pleasure to show you my suite, Mr. Harvest," he said. He stood up, helped Rirha to her feet and waddled off with her towards the lift. I followed immediately behind.

His smile was bland as the lift moved upwards. The Arab woman was looking me up and down, slightly contemptuous.

The lift glided to a halt at the third floor. I followed them out and along the corridor. We entered a luxuriously furnished suite, passing through a private hall into a large lounge. When Rirha was seated, Zarouk asked me to sit down and rang a bell. I moved across the room and sat with my back against a wall.

A moment later, an inner door opened and three massive Arabs entered.

Zarouk was smiling like a Siamese cat.

"How very foolish of you, Mr. Harvest, to put yourself in my hands for punishment! I am sure that Miss bent Ali will be very grateful to you for the spectacle. On the other hand, she has a delicate taste for blood!"

"Perhaps Meester 'Arvest is sorry he is come?" said Rirha in her rich passionate voice.

I grinned.

"I'd send these turkeys away before they get hurt if I were you," I said lazily.

Underneath, however, I was bracing myself for the attack.

Zarouk spoke some words in Arabic, quickly, so that I was unable to catch what he said, but there was

no time for doubt because the three men were closing in on me.

I delayed for a fraction of a second longer, and
then, swivelling the chair from underneath me, I
rammed it into the face of the man nearest me.
Simultaneously, the others threw themselves at me. I
was quick enough to meet one of them with a violent
knee thrust to the groin. He slinked away with a
howl of pain. The third meanwhile had his huge
hands on my throat and the bleeding face of the man
whom I had hit with the chair was advancing
towards me from the side. I removed my strangler by
a quick blow of my hand under his nose, and as his
head tilted backwards my hand struck like a blunt
knife on his Adam's apple. At that moment, I was
toppled off my feet by the man with the bleeding
face. We rolled over on the carpet in a bear hug.
Unhurriedly, my fingers sought the nerve-center
behind his ear. I pressed with all the force of my
thumb. He screamed and relaxed his grip. I twisted
him on his front and knocked him unconscious with
a vicious blow to the back of his neck. I was up in
time to kick the man, whom I had injured in the
groin. My foot connected with his teeth as he strug-
gled with me. His head hit the carpeted floor with a
thud. I hesitated, but the attack was not renewed. I
dusted myself off and told Zarouk to put his ridiculous pistol away.

Rirha let out a silvery peal of laughter.

Zarouk threw a viperous look in her direction and
held his pistol aimed towards me.

I walked over to the cocktail cabinet, poured
myself a drink, lit a cigarette, and, turning to face
him, said:

"Where is Miss Dalton?"

"You fool!" he snarled. "Do you think I'll tell you

124

where the bitch is? Sit on that chair over there! Quick!"

I didn't move. I grinned at him.

"Don't upset yourself, Zarouk," I said. "You're an old man...a dirty old man!"

For a moment I thought I had gone too far. His knuckle whitened on the trigger. Rirha drew in her breath. And then, as I prepared to throw myself out of the way, there was a useless click. He had forgotten to remove the safety catch. I hesitated no longer. While he was still gazing down at the unexploded revolver, I threw myself across the room, wrested it from his grasp and brought my knee up with all my force into his pot belly. The breath issued from his gaping face in a long painful wheeze. He changed color, tottered unsteadily forward, sank to his knees, and, a moment later, on all fours, crouched on the plush carpet. I stood back and watched him gasp for breath.

"I should kill you, you fat slob," I said gently. "Take a shot at me again and I'll carve you into little pieces!"

Zarouk probably didn't hear. He was still bent over as I turned away and moved across to where Rirha bent Ali had settled herself on the settee.

"Perhaps you can tell me where Miss Dalton is?" I said to her.

"Of course," she said softly, "but let me give you some advice, Meester 'Arvest."

"Sure," I said with a grin.

"You should take Miss Dalton far away from here, away from Africa, tonight, tomorrow at the latest."

"So?"

"You are a ver' brave man, Meester 'Arvest. But you are too young to die. Why don't you go 'ome like a good boy?"

125

"That will be difficult after seeing you," I cracked.

"That is impossible, Meester 'Arvest. And now, if you will take my advice, you will go next door and take Mees Dalton away before Zarouk has 'is revenge."

Without replying I moved quickly into the inner room where I found Rosemary in some kind of coma in a large double bed. She looked beautiful, her long fair hair straggling across the pillows, the white rise of her taut and naked breasts visible just below the sheets. I slipped down the covers and admired her. A red weal running downward from her sculpted hip under her buttocks caught my eye. I turned her over. Someone had flogged her with a thin cane. My mouth tightened. I wondered whether she had submitted to this of her own accord or whether Zarouk had taken advantage of her.

However, there was no time for a post mortem. I dressed her quickly, first making sure that the door between the rooms was locked, and then raised her to her feet. She was in a semi-conscious state. They had evidently drugged her.

Automatic in hand, I reopened the door.

Zarouk had recovered. All but one of the Arabs was gone. Zarouk himself, looking ill, was seated again, and his pale eyes surveyed me coldly as I entered. Rirha was lying at full length on the settee. She was smiling.

"We have decided to let you go…" Zarouk began.

"Listen, my little raton," I said pleasantly, "you don't let me do anything. Next time you get in my way, I'll leave a permanent mark on you, savvy?"

He looked at me dangerously.

Rirha interrupted him before he could speak.

"You will leave Africa tomorrow, Meester 'Arvest. You weel both take the plane at 6:15 P.M. After that, I shall not interfere. Zarouk will keel you."

"This goes for you too," I said, turning on her. "Don't get in my way, Rirha. Otherwise, you won't be fit for a camel."

Her eyes sparkled angrily. Zarouk almost stood up, but the effort was too much for him. He sat back with a stifled groan of pain. On the way out I turned my attention to the Arab who was bending over cleaning up the mess we'd made during the struggle. I let fly with one foot, catching him on the fat part of his buttocks and sending him sprawling headlong across the floor.

"And if you value these dogs, keep them well out of my sight. In future I'm going to be much rougher with them."

With that, I steadied Rosemary and walked out into the hall with her.

Outside, we took a taxi back to the hotel.

Chapter 5

The roar of the plane died away overhead. I watched it then, a small bird speeding swiftly outward towards the Mediterranean. In it went Rosemary, who, the ·previous night, had lain in my arms, warm, supple, soft, submissive after her experience at the hands of Zarouk. For a while she had lain still in my arms, tremulous, naked, almost more naked and exposed than it is possible for a woman to be. Zarouk's cruelty had shattered her. And I was so presumptuous to think the fat, nasty Egyptian would free her sexually—when it was me all along who was to play that role. I brought back the woman in her with a patient and gentle caress. It was not long before she responded, but when she did so, it was as though her limbs were weighted with lead. Her body cried out for tender love, her voice huskily called on me to arouse her. The woman I had fantasized about, the beautiful blond who I imagined gamahuching the Arab cigarette girl and fucking the fat Egyptian, needed TLC—and she needed it from me! When I touched her bruises, she quivered, but almost with pleasure, and when we made love, her limbs lifted themselves with heavy determinism into gentle suggestion. She was very beautiful.

The minute I got her back to the hotel and away from the fat Egyptian, I knew I would treat her gently, kindly, with my deepest compassion—and passions—for her foray into what was to be a forbidden lust became a foray into pain and fear when Zarouk not only fucked her from behind like a dog, but caned her as he rode her, whipping her behind and the skin of her hip, as he got his kicks from coming quickly inside her and seeing both his come drip from between her legs, and the welts raise on her flesh.

I kissed and touched those bruises gently, which is why it made her shiver with a pleasurable feeling. And I massaged her shoulders, her arms, her legs, her neck, and brought her back to life from the drugs he had knocked her out with. Seeing she was so weak, so laden down, I left the moves of love to her…and it wasn't until she asked me for it that I gave her the great pleasure of my fondness for her.

First, I kissed the lovely pink nipple buds and softly molded and moved the tender breasts in my hands, and then I kissed the flat of her stomach, the bruises on her side, the skin on her inner thigh.

I kissed my way back to her lips, and there, we French kissed for long, luxurious moments, sucking one another's tongues, probing the insides of each other's mouths, kissing as the heat between our legs, between our bodies, began to build.

I knew how much it meant to her to be loved this

way, and it made my cock hard just to know how vulnerable she really was, and how much she trusted me to care for her, to love her up, to protect her. There was a part of me that wanted to bury my cock deep into the canal of her cunt, and stay there, filling her, fulfilling her. But first, I traveled down the length of her body with my tongue and my kissing caresses and came upon the soft, furry mound of golden hair. In all my fantasies and thoughts of Rosemary Dalton, I had not yet been this close to the inner sanctum of love—I'd only imagined it.

I burrowed my face into the soft, flaxen hairs and lightly kissed the salty dew that clung to them. Her legs, quite naturally, opened to me then and there I was taken, so wonderfully taken and awed, by the beautiful sight of the pink pussy petals of flesh that hid beneath the cunt fuzz, between the perfectly long, lithe legs of the vulnerable, beautiful creature.

Now, my lips bent to the folds, so brightly pink and softly fleshy. My tongue searched out the now-protruding love bud, the swelling clit that I immediately took between my lips, sucking and kissing the swollen gland.

Her legs spread even further apart, and now, she was moaning, oohing and ahhing, and spreading herself more and more open, until finally, her legs so far apart, I could see clearly the deep, pink crevice that led the way to her womb and could see the pearly droplets of love juice beginning to wet the outer rim. I pressed my lips to the pussyhole, and kissed it, then slid my tongue in half way, then all the way, and began to explore the depths of her cunt with deep, probing motions of my tongue. I was in love with the juicy taste of her, the soft velvet feel of her insides on my tongue, and the way she began to press her pussy upward into my mouth. My tongue, at certain points, was buried inside her to the teeth, and this meant my lips were then wide open and pressed upon her cunt lips and I could have the whole of her fleshy pussy lips in my mouth, while filling her up with my tongue.

She writhed in ecstasy as I moved to the engorged clit bud, a sweet pink mound of sensual flesh. I licked it, and she moaned. I pressed my mouth over it, took it inward, sucked it upward and felt it in my mouth like a delicious piece of candy.

With my hands, I spread her open wider, using my thumbs to press the little clit bud from under its shell and give me complete, utter access.

I was ravenous for her cunt, eating and sucking her deliriously, until I started to feel the shudder of her orgasm coming on, and felt her heaving her hips into my mouth. I sucked longer, deeper, wetter sucks of her clit as I felt the come stirring through her in the first contractions.

She was breathing heavily, and with all her energy she grabbed hold of my head and pressed my face firmly to her clit as she wrapped her legs around my head while the orgasm rocked through her ovaries. She was trembling with joy and with weakness as the soft ejaculations of pussy juice began to squirt into my mouth. Her legs soon stopped their motion, and her cunt was done contracting. I slipped my tongue deep into the slash between her legs and licked the last drops of her jism, the taste a tangy delight on my tongue.

I kissed her sweet cunt, and laid my head upon the long, silky leg. My cock was bursting with passion, but I thought she needed a rest. I was surprised when she urged me to gently fill her with my manhood.

I lifted myself over her, and my hard cock immediately found its way to the silky entrance to her cunt. I pressed in, slowly at first, filling her with anticipation as I held her at bay for a moment by placing just the head of my cock into the front of her hatch. She lay there, awaiting my next move and was thrilled when she felt me fill her to the core with a deep, swift thrust.

I pulled out, perched at the cunt opening again, and pressed inward—thrusting myself up against her womb again. She was totally receptive, totally surrendered to me, as I made love to her, and we soon were making love like one single organism, my cock, her cunt, part of the same moment in time.

Her cunt lips swelled up with pleasure quickly, and literally strangled the come out of my throbbing member.

As the contractions of pleasure took hold of me, I could feel her quickly catch up as wave after wave after wave of excitement washed over her and brought down the copious emissions of her cunt.

I had nothing but warm feelings for her when we said goodbye at the airport.

I turned away from the disappearing plane with the knowledge that my enemies had witnessed Rosemary's departure to Paris. They were also well aware that I had not left with her.

I was wearing my weapons. A small Mauser in my side pocket, a Luger in a shoulder holster, my little stick of rubber-covered lead in my sleeve and a razor blade sewn into my cuff. I walked deliberately back to the passengers' bar, ordered a whiskey, and surveyed the large room in the mirror. For the most part, the people were obviously passengers; tourists with sun hats, sweating French businessmen, women with high-pitched voices. I looked for my man.

He was standing not far from me at the other end of the bar. Like most hired watch dogs, he had an uncanny capacity for being obvious. He was pretending to be thoughtful, an Arab in European clothes, rather ugly. I finished my drink, slipped off the stool, and walked across to him. I smiled as I approached. He looked startled.

"Zarouk send you?" I said with a grin.

"I don't know what you mean," he said sullenly in French.

I put my hand in my pocket and touched the Mauser that was hidden there against his back. He could feel its blunt nose through the material.

"Let's get out of here," I said.

He hesitated. I jabbed him hard in the ribs with the hidden gun. Then he stood up, paid for his drink and walked out ahead of me. We walked over to where a black sedan was parked. At one glance I noticed that there was only one other man in the interior. He was in the driver's seat. I opened the door and told the ugly one to get in beside his friend. Then I slipped into the back seat, produced my gun, and told the driver to return to town. In that way, with my pursuers in front of me, I was able to have a pleasant journey.

I slipped out of the car at a crossing and darted into a side street before my fellow passengers had time to halt the car. They moved forward in a wave of traffic, helpless to prevent me.

Next, I phoned the hotel, told them to send my bags at once to the railway station, and that I would settle my bill there. Then I took a taxi to the station, bought a ticket for Ghardaia, and waited for my bags to arrive. About fifteen minutes later, one of the desk clerks came into the waiting room with a wide smile. He was carrying my bags. I paid my bill, tipped him, and boarded the train.

I sat with my back to the engine and watched the platform for a possible pursuer. Nothing happened for twenty minutes and then, just before the train pulled out, a single Arab sidled along the platform and boarded the train. I fixed his picture in my memory, eased the holster at my shoulder, and fell into a doze.

I slept for perhaps an hour and then, waking up with the darkening countryside spreading backwards away from the window, I pulled the blinds, switched on the light in the carriage and composed myself to write a little verse. I wrote as follows:

FIRST LOVE

I was like she was, hot see?
a fat lovable little boy
with an eye
that peeped at her, what she showed
with sheer joy
the slicks, flats
elastic tensions at her great
her imperial thighs

the torque
of her hot delta which
smoked a Turkish cigarette
for me to see
that she was all lips and hips
at the base of the green pod
the raised skirt
she burgeoned downward from
like a shining bean

well, at that point
her belly dangling like
an egg on poach
she scissored her legs cleverly
and spat out the roach
which I raised to my lips

I was like she was, fat, see?
and she at her ease
one hand on her hip and ripe
was she as (a thumb-press
on) a Camembert cheese
her chevron gamey-dark
like good game as she came on me
and retrieved her cigarette

which like a flutist
she laid at her mouth, inhaled
and threw it away
before she leaned against me
like a sea

I was like she was, bare, see?
a hot, improbable little boy
with an eye
that peeped at her, what she showed
with sheer joy

the sprouts, teats
sun-dried figs at her great
her queenly globes

the slack of her thick muscle as she breathed
the settling of her pores
for me to smell
that she was all sweets and sweats
at her considerable surfaces
the furled flag
red, as tautly she leaned backwards on
the groaning bed
well, at this point
she 'collected' me, as to her
as a windy skirt
her knees fell open tidily
and I horsed her cart.

I read it over with pleasure. I would send it to

Nadya who, I felt sure, would appreciate it. I laid it on the seat beside me and lit a cigarette.

The train appeared to have stopped at a small station. I moved to pull the blind aside but then I changed my mind and sat back comfortably in the corner. A moment later, there was a knock on the door of the compartment and a well-shaped woman of forty entered. She was a European. She carried one small red leather bag which she appeared to have some difficulty in putting on the rack. I rose at once and aided her. As I did so, my papers, which had been lying on the seat beside me fell on to the floor. Thus as I came downward from the rack I met her coming upwards with my papers which she handed across to me.

"Thank you very much," she said in English with a slight middle-European accent. "So kind!"

At that moment, her eyes caught sight of the poetry, and taking the papers from my hands, said, "You write poetry, Monsieur?" and settled back in the corner opposite me to study what I had written.

I grinned and settled back opposite her. If she was going to be shocked she deserved it. But certainly, if she was, she gave no evidence of it.

Instead she demanded: "What is precisely this word 'teats', monsieur?"

"Precisely nipples," I replied sweetly.

She smiled.

"Is it not rather risqué, this poem?"

"Some might find it so," I replied gravely.

"You love women, then?"

I was rather taken aback by her directness.

"Some women," I said pleasantly.

She smiled. Then she crossed over and sat down beside me, taking my hand in hers. "And you could love me?" she said, her eyes shining.

She smelled very interesting. She was what is called a 'mature' woman, that is to say, one whose body has thickened perceptibly from love making over a score of years. It occurred to me that the seed of all races had probably met in her belly, the invaders of a hundred situations, times, appetites, and there is a peculiar fascination in such a belly, that it should have moistened to countless men, the strength of the thighs and the wholeheartedness of the lust increasing as the woman flung every meaningless inhibition aside and gave herself, 'coarsening' (they call it), to the other belly which is inspired by the lust it feeds upon.

"Nothing would give me more pleasure," I said truthfully and I allowed my right hand to lay itself tentatively on the bulge of her warm thigh over which the soft wool of the dress was stretched in diagonal ruts.

"The lights," she said softly.

I rose and switched them out.

As I moved backwards like a blind man to find her, I felt myself drawn quickly to a position on my knees on the floor, and, before I could protest against or abet the movement, my head was drawn inexorably under her skirt, upwards, my cheeks brushing against her delicately unshaven thighs, until my mouth was pressed against her broad and secret weal of flesh and hair on which her passion stood out in sudden beads of moisture. I allowed myself to be used in that way, conniving with her by opening my mouth in an attempt to contain her and at the same time thrusting my tongue in the viscid whirlpool of her ecstasy. Soon she had bared her broad belly and was rubbing my face against it, my head held by the hair in the strong forceps of her fingers. I kissed and licked its soft tremulous surface. She was breathing heavily, her thighs clamping me around my chest.

From under her skirt, I played with the plump, wrinkled pussy lips and caressed her belly. Pulling her underwear to the side, I liked her clit, which seemed more wrinkled and puckered than most of the younger cunts I'd had, but which hardened just the same to the feel of my tongue washing over it.

The woman moaned and pressed her hands down on my head, pushing my face deep into the crevice between her legs. My tongue easily found the hole and with the help of my fingers to spread it open, I began to eat her with great joy, loving the taste of this new cunt, and the fact that she so openly wanted me.

I imagined what it would be like to ram her with my hard cock, press her up against a wall or put her on the floor and fill that big, wet hole with my big, aching piece of male meat.

I wanted to fuck her; I was hard for her, and my cock was ready to burst. I had to put it somewhere, fill someone with it.

I attempted then to lift the lower part of her torso and myself onto the seat but she resisted.

"Wait!" she whispered. "It is not safe here, *chéri.* There is no lock on the door. Come to the toilet."

I stood up rather reluctantly and adjusted my tie which was threatening to strangle me. At the same moment her skirts came down and she stood beside me and kissed me on the lips.

"It will be better there," she said softly.

"The floor is hard. There is nothing but wood, stone, and metal!"

I grinned and grasped her buttocks ungently close.

"Wait!" She was smiling. "And now come!"

We walked quickly along the deserted corridor to the toilet. She opened the door and allowed me to pass in first. As I did so, I heard a swishing sound, hesitated, and then crumpled to my knees with a cry of pain as the blackjack struck me on the temple...and I lost consciousness.

When I came to, I was lying on my belly beside the railroad track. I woke with the dawn, a splitting pain at the back of my skull. When I touched my right temple I could feel the caked blood which had run in streams down my cheek. There was something wrong with my left wrist and the flesh of my left hip, bruised and grazed, showed through a tear in my trousers. My hands went automatically to my pockets. They were all empty. My wallet, my papers, and the various weapons had been taken from me. With a curse, my hand went under my shirt to feel for my concealed money belt. Fortunately, it was still there next to my skin. Guns could be replaced, papers were not strictly necessary, but the power to bribe and buy services was imperative.

The landscape was pretty bleak: a few scrubs, date palms, and a few tilled fields, an ochre color, with a small hut at the far side, were all that was visible at my side of the railway embankment on which I had been thrown from the train.

From where I was lying I could see a few white-cloaked figures already up and about near the huts. To stand up was painful, but after a few efforts I managed to raise myself to my feet and stumble across the rough scrub-covered grounds towards them. A group of people watched my approach. I went forward.

"*Salam Aleykum!*" I said in greeting to one of the older men who stood near the front of the group.

He returned my greeting gravely and then, when I was quite close, he signed for the group to make way and led me into one of the huts.

I sat on a cushion on top of some sheep skins.

He, meanwhile, had produced a long spouted silver teapot and was brewing mint tea. It was not until he had poured it into two little glasses on a silver tray that he spoke.

He spoke first in Arabic, some of which I understood but most of which went over my head, and then, when he saw I was having difficulties with the language, he began to talk a kind of pigeon French. How had I come to be there? Where was I going? Could he be of any small service to me? All the while he remained grave and kind.

I told him that some enemies of mine had thrown me from the train in the middle of the night after taking all my papers.

"The train for Ghardaia?" I nodded.

"And you still wish to go to Ghardaia?"

I nodded again. And then slowly, half in Arabic and half in French, I explained that I would like to buy a burnoose and, if possible, some weapons. I told him I wished to travel on to Ghardaia as quickly as possible.

He assured me that he would do everything in his power to help me, but I had the impression that his idea of urgency and mine were poles apart. He told me that he had a nephew who lived in Ghardaia. The nephew's name was Mohan ben Abdelahman and he was some kind of merchant in the city. His uncle assured me that when I gave his nephew the letter which he would give me for him, his nephew would give me all the assistance in his power. Nevertheless, in view of the fact that my business was against the interests of the chief of the territory, Hussein ben Ali, I decided that it would be unwise to acquaint my host with its nature. I asked him instead how long it would take me to reach Ghardaia.

His answer was vague. In Europe or America information of that kind will be precise to within a few minutes or a few hours depending on the length of the journey. In the Arab countries, time is of such an abstract nature, it is hardly distinguished from the living. He assured me merely that it was not far and, try as I would, I could not get him to be more explicit. Would somebody act as my guide? Of course, he would arrange that. I could set out on the following day. Meanwhile, I should accept his hospitality. I should rest and try to recover as much as possible from the blows I had sustained at the hands of my enemies.

I asked him again about getting arms.

He himself, he said, had a Mauser automatic, and he had no doubt that we could come to some arrangement about it. Meanwhile, however, I should sleep.

I said that I would do so but that I would like to smoke some 'kief' to make the passage of time until the next day more pleasant. He smiled and a moment later brought a long pipe to me and a little pouch in which some of the drug was contained. When I had packed and lit the pipe, he watched until I had drawn the first few clouds of the sweet smoke into my lungs, and then, without a word, he went outside. I smoked one pipeful and then a second, but before I had finished it I fell into a deep sleep.

I felt thoroughly refreshed when I awoke. Pausing only to light a cigarette, I lay back again amongst the cushions and looked back over the series of events which had occurred since I had arrived in North Africa. After going over them once, I made a list of names as follows:

Colonel Jerome Poilu

Hussein ben Ali
Rirha bent Ali
Abdelkader ben Tahar (pimp)
Mr. Zarouk

As far as I could see, these were the only five people who mattered and it was probable that any one of them could give me much of the information I required. Of one thing I was now quite certain: Helen Seferis was still alive. On no other plausible theory could I explain the anxiety of my enemies to get rid of me.

But that was not all. My mind flew back to my interview with Mr. Borthese. I remembered my saying: "She was taken by caravan for weeks across desert! They went south obviously, roughly speaking towards Tamanrasset, Touareg country."

And I remembered his laconic reply: "It is quite obvious that you know as much about it as we do in Algiers. I suggest that the only person who can give you further information is Colonel Poilu himself." It seemed to me now that I had been on the wrong track. That was the point of Mr. Borthese's irony. If Helen Seferis were safely in Touareg country, it was hardly probable that the above quintet would be at such pains to hinder the movements of a lone private detective in the vicinity of Ghardaia. Their anxiety to get rid of me, therefore, led me to my next thesis: Helen Seferis was somewhere in or near Ghardaia and for some reason best known to themselves these five people were interested in keeping her whereabouts secret. That could only mean, further, that Helen Seferis was being held against her will.

In the light of the manuscript which I had now lost, that was an interesting piece of information. Her manuscript had ended with a triumphal acceptance of the strange sexual situation in which she had become immersed. Something, then, had occurred to make her change her mind. What?

I remembered particularly one sentence in her testimony:

"And gradually the whole desire to commit my experiences to history has been outflanked by the terrible pleasure I experience in approaching the unconscious state of an object, an amorphous mass of sensitive flesh and fibre with the form of will."

and again:

"The comings and goings of my lovers are merely the gentle showers which nurture the plant...the plant is myself, living on and on with a slow stirring motion through nights and days and nights and days of voluptuousness..."

Such a state, induced by the combination of drugs and hothouse sex, is not easily broken down. If it had continued as she described it, she would have no motive to disrupt the cloying pleasure of her days and nights in the exotic brothel. What could have made her change her mind?

Without further hesitation, I underlined the names of Hussein ben Ali and Mr. Zarouk. The pimp, ben Tahar, was obviously a pawn. He had kept his mouth closed under orders. The Frenchman, Poilu, if I went by the information already gathered, was fully occupied by the sensual charms of Rirha bent Ali.

I am not a cynic. There was no political motive for the abduction of Helen Seferis. That left one motive, one which fitted, that of sex. It seemed, therefore, that Helen Seferis had been dragged unwillingly from the vast dream world in which she had become involved to occupy the bed of one of two men, Sheikh Hussein ben Ali himself, or the ambiguous Mr. Zarouk. And the fact that Rirha bent Ali had used her charms to ensure the cooperation of the police official, Poilu, suggested that I wouldn't have to look much farther than the harem of the Sheikh himself.

I was pleased with my analysis. I starred the name of the Sheikh and put a question mark at the name of Mr. Zarouk. There remained only the tinkling out of a plan of action. An obvious one suggested itself. I would tackle the weakest link first. I smiled when I thought that Abdelkader ben Tahar had no suspicion of what was in store for him. He would find my questioning more persuasive than that of either Colonel Poilu or the conventional Mr. Linklater.

Lying backwards on the cushions again, I lit the pipe and drew a deep breath.

A short while later my host returned with some stewed mutton and a varied assortment of sweetmeats, dates, figs, and crushed almonds. I ate with relish in his presence.

He asked me how I felt and I replied that I had quite recovered. He seemed pleased about this and, a moment later, asked me if I would care to join him in an evening's entertainment. A caravan had arrived, it appeared, which would stay the night at the village and then move onwards to the west. The villagers considered themselves fortunate indeed because a group of musicians and belly dancers was travelling with the caravan and a dance was at that moment being arranged. He said that the women were ravishing and young and that he did not think it would be difficult to arrange to make love with them. He noted my interest with evident satisfaction and we left the hut together and walked across to the large, brightly colored tent which the musicians had erected. Music already issued from it, the strange breaking quail of

rhaita (flûte) and voice, with the primitive harpsi-
chord quality of fiddle accompaniment.

The tent was already crowded with people who
clapped their hands to the beat of the music and a
man in a yellow blouse with a magnificent red beard
was singing a duet with a frail saucer-eyed girl who
looked alternatively at the ground and at the wall of
the tent above as her full quavering voice issued from
her throat.

When the song was over, we moved forward and
seated ourselves at the edge of the circle into which a
plump Arab woman of about twenty-eight had come
to begin a belly dance. The chucks of her flesh quivered voluptuously at her belly and thighs, and her
breasts, sustained flatly above her oiled and gleaming
belly by a red band of silk, shuddered like blanc-
mange in response to the strong and sinuous torso
movements which electrified the smoky atmosphere
and held the pale, lustful eyes of the men. She
stamped and sweated, her bare feet striking the carpet and raising dust like soft hammers. Her belly
swayed like a moon of whitish gold, or like the pale
yoke of an egg, dangling in a frame of soft passionate
muscle which fell smoothly across her heavy hips.
Her navel was obscured by a little red cluster of
sequins which drew brilliance from the oil lamps and
radiated a hundred transparent spears of red light in
every direction. Her sex was obscured (or almost, for
a frail fringe of blue-black hair was visible on her
lower belly), by a sort of helio drape which fell downward from her body's center to somewhere just below
her knees. The same drape clung smoothly about her
haunches and fell at the back almost to ground level.

Her face was broad with high cheekbones and the
flashing black eyes above them had been treated with
kohl to give them that deep-set, other-worldly

appearance. Her mouth was big with thick lustful lips from which, as she stamped her foot like a mare in heat, her crude deep voice issued suggestively, and all the time her belly quivered, advanced and retreated, gathered itself, and threw itself like wind in a white sail outward, exposing still more of the blue-black hairs of her sex.

My companion nudged me and said that this was Zora, a woman of the interior, who would make a great name for herself in a city cabaret. I expressed my wholehearted admiration for her and he, laughing slightly in his beard, said that if it pleased me I might be able to spend the night with her. It would be costly but, in his opinion, worth it. I agreed with him. Would he make the arrangements? He said he would look into it as soon as the dance was over for he was afraid by the look of the men that there might be some competition for her favors. I told him not to worry about the price and it amused me to think that I would put it to expenses when I sent Nadya her bill. Having smoked sufficient *kief* to stimulate every urgent sinew of my solar plexus, I had no wish to lose the voluptuous Zora to another. As soon as her dance was over, I walked out of the tent and stood out in the open, smoking a cigarette. Outside in the soft darkness I waited for my host to return with news of the assignation.

I was smoking another pipe when she entered. She was dressed entirely as she had danced, the cluster of ruby-colored sequins at her navel and the helio drape shrouding the heavy sexuality of her haunches. She stood smiling in the doorway, the bead curtain behind her, as though waiting to be invited to enter. I signed to her and she walked slowly towards me with thick, rhythmic movements. Her belly was still,

147

almost motionless above the shrouded movement of
her thighs, and I was aware for the first time as she
came close to me that her plump and rippling body
exuded a strong odor of woman. That odor, overpowering as it sometimes is in a room full of chorus girls,
was under the effect of the drug perhaps the most
seductive thing about her. It synchronized in some
primal way with the long and powerful walls of flesh
that compacted her hot lustful body. She was such a
woman as few white men ever possess, a woman who
would always seem out of place in a Westernized
salon, a woman who could cause nothing but shock
and uneasiness because of the coarse, sudden, earth-
struck quality of her movements, her body oiled, the
oil, a heavy odor in itself, mingling with the generous
sweat of her thighs and armpits, her thick blue-black
hair greased until it shone, her eyes blackened with
kohl, her clothes worn frankly only to emphasize the
creamy vastness of her supple abdomen; they were,
from a Western point of view, not clothes at all, and
yet, as I realized from the beginning, they were all
she had, seemed adequate to her, for the simple reason that it had never occurred to her that a woman
could be anything other than an instrument of love
for a man. She squatted beside me without hesitation, and as, from my reclining position on the cushions, my eyes fell from her savage head down over
the pulpy cloth-draped breasts to the restful heap of
her hair-trimmed belly, I watched her right hand
move under the lower drape and knead, almost
reflectively, at the thick and sullen flesh of her thigh.
When I looked up again, she was smiling, but in such
a way that it was impossible to know what she was
thinking.

I was in no hurry to have her. I was amazed at the
strength of the soft, almost fetid, flesh in repose.

Half an hour before, I had witnessed its ecstatic shudder which had struck me at the time as very close to the sudden and shocking twitch of a cat's fur when it is startled by something unknown; the primitiveness of that movement had had the effect of putting me in direct electric contact with something towards which I felt myself gravitate relentlessly. I wanted, as the drug rose again to my head, to be devoured by her massive thighs, to sink utterly into the seam of lips that appeared now, under wet hairs, as her hand untied the helio veil which sank to the ground around the shining bowl of her tawny haunches.

I leaned over and pulled her towards me. She came without resistance but at the same time without connivance. I laid her face upwards across my knees so that her heavy body was bent backwards like a bow, head and hair on the ground at one side and her feet on the ground at the other, balanced across my knees on the small of her back. I moved her slightly then so that the hot naked weight of her buttocks came to repose on top of my hidden member, and then, almost as though she were the keyboard of a piano, I felt the snug mounds of flesh with the tips of my fingers. I explored every crevice, every thick and oiled under-run of flesh and muscle, between her thighs, at her armpits, under her ribcage, and finally with the fingers of my right hand, the tight rolls of fat which made the meat of her powerful mound. The hairs were wiry, strong-odored, and glistening with the juices that her lust brought to my caress. Looking down between them, her thighs fell away in their flatness to the twin bunches of her gleaming buttocks between which, in a crisscross of matted hair, the yellow furrow ran down and inward the round ring of her second sex, loose yet definitive as a foal's nostril. I inserted my fingers in such a way that I held her by two cavities, raising the arch of her body upwards to my lips so that she was supported like a bridge-span by her feet and shoulders. At that moment her knees slewed open and her sex opened about my fingers like a jaw.

I slipped from under her and took off my own clothes. She was lying on the ground now, gazing indolently upwards with her dark eyes at my increasing sex, and then, as I moved naked towards her, she rose to her knees and grasping me about the waist drew the rod to her lips which broke open over it until it was contained to the hilt in the soft wetness within.

I allowed her to devour it for a few moments, and then, taking her by the hair, I twisted her backwards in front of me and, with my right foot between her now naked breasts, I heaved her with all my force backwards so that she sprawled headlong across the hut. I waited until she landed, her belly upwards and her legs apart, and then, bracing myself for a leap, I threw myself horizontally into the air and landed with a fleshy crash along the length of her voluptuously rising front. This had the effect of knocking the breath out of her momentarily, but didn't prevent her from uttering an oath and writhing like a snake in my grasp. I felt her strong teeth bite into my shoulder as my rod crushed through the softened undergrowth that tipped her lower belly. Meanwhile, I had pinioned her hands with my own, making a quivering crucifix of our lust, and, as my belly nudged softly as on ballbearings on hers. I felt her heavy, sweated thighs open and contain my trunk like a vise.

She heaved those huge hips upward to greet my thrusting rod, and I pummeled myself deep into the folds of her fat cunt, feeling the great release of a day of torturous physical abuse and annoyance. And here was my prize, a big-boned, fleshy-bodied total woman whose very purpose was to be there for my pleasure, and yet whose feisty nature compelled her to play a fair game in love and war; suddenly, she seized me, and took over the lead for our fuck.

She pushed me from between her legs, rolled me over on my back, took hold of my hard cock and pressed her lips down on the rampant rod while jerking it from the base and fondling my balls, bringing me close to the breaking point. Wetting a middle finger, she found the narrow gateway to my anal canal, and pressed herself into my tight, rarely touched asshole, charging in like someone who has the key to the city and no longer asks permission if she can use it!

I spread my legs apart and let her finger fuck my butt, and let her suck my member into the depths of her throat, and relaxed into the role of being dominated by one who was big enough and strong enough, to be in charge.

Now she was ready for a fuck—her style—and she hoisted a huge thigh over my legs, squatted her cunt right above my hard cock, and impaled herself upon my prick.

She rode me like I was some animal, there for her use, and crashed her fat snatch down upon me, fucking me like a wild woman in heat.

She bent over and began to nibble at my neck, bite my shoulder, and suck my nipples, all the while she was grinding that huge, gaping cunt hole against my cock.

Her breath turned into a panting, groaning, grunting noise and I could feel the large, swelled cunt lips getting tighter around my cock.

As she pressed her pussy down atop the mound of my groin, panting into my chest, she shoved one huge, dangling tit into my mouth as I began to suck it with all the passion of a lover who wanted nothing but to pleasure his Queen.

The fleshy ass was coming down harder now, slapping against my balls, as she fucked me and I sucked her, bringing her close to an explosive climax.

She was intentionally tightening the muscles at the ring of her snatch around my pole, trying to get me to come with her, when suddenly I felt the strong, brown fingers move around my waist, down to my butt beneath her and, with javelin-like force, thrust into my asshole.

She rammed me with those fingers, pressing herself in mercilessly, as if those fingers were another man's cock trying to penetrate the soul of my maleness. And suddenly, I felt myself become dizzy with the whirring feel of a beginning orgasm rushing through my groin. The heady scent of her orifices, her womanhood, and her body odor, combined with her wild, wanton fucking and her fingers imbedded in my ass, were winning me over. Suddenly, I felt myself about to burst into the warm, vacant womb of the fleshy, brown-skinned woman.

And she, too, was coming near the climax, as her cunt was twitching wildly with the contractions of pleasure. Then her mouth was at mine, crushing, biting, and savoring the taste of our tongues rubbing against one another as our bellies did the same. We thrashed our spasms at one another's groins, the come dripping from us both like a faucet of jism. She fell atop me in a heap of sexual flesh, spent, complete—having pleased me and pleasured herself in the process.

I would have given a great deal to be able to take

her back with me to the fogs of London. She would have improved the tone of my glass room immensely and have made an excellent whore-mistress for such delicate little friends of mine as Sybil Batterram.

Chapter 6

I always need a prison. I don't mean an ordinary police jail where they hold men when they don't know what to do with them, I mean something more akin to a morgue or an undertaker's parlor where it is evident what is going to happen to the prisoner after certain physical operations have been made upon him. On the other hand, not all my prisoners come out in a box. Some walk out unhurt, others scarred, others more or less maimed for life, depending upon the degree to which they were cooperative during their 'cures'. I am not a sadistic man by habit. When I am sadistic, it is because I have chosen to be so. I am nonetheless no Robin Hood. If you see my car parked near a Boy Scout camp, it will not be because I have taken a sudden interest in camping but more probably because I have taken a sudden interest in boys. What I am laboring to make you understand is that the 'prison' is an indispensable function in my detecting system. This system is, of course, inevitably colored by my emotional make-up.

The principles underlying my system of detection are as follows:

(1) Detecting is a job like any other, painful at best, necessary for economic reasons. Make it pay.

(2) The less time you spend at detecting the better. Invent shortcuts.

The individually devised principles under Section (2) are as follows:

    (a) Take risks. The other man won't.

    (b) Cut sentiment, that's to say 'morals'.

Finally, and as an example of what I mean: Don't waste your time following a man: beat him over the head with a club and ask him where he was going.

And that brings me back to my 'prison'. You wonder perhaps why I took the trouble to write down five names? I was (according to my system) drawing up my 'roll-call'. These were five people who risked to visit me for a cure in what, according to their degree of cooperativeness, would prove to be their 'playpen', their 'hospital', or their 'morgue'. I find the system practical, sanitary, and in all ways time-saving. I arrive with due thought to the extent of my 'roll-call', select my first actual prisoner from amongst their number, and the wickets (to adopt the vocabulary of my dear friend, Mrs. Batterram) fall fast and thick until I have solved the 'mystery'. The use of unorthodox methods, moreover, allows me to compete successfully enough with the police; that is the source of my fortune.

My first act when I arrived, in Arab clothes, in the tent-scattered precincts of Ghardaia (I drove in finally on a bus) was to look up the nephew of my host at the Arab village. He was a 'Hadj'—which is to say he had made the prescribed pilgrimage to Mecca—as well as a well-to-do merchant in the town of Ghardaia. He greeted me with great politeness when he heard I came from his uncle and he assured me that he would do whatever he could to make my stay safe and pleasant. I nearly gave in to one of his suggestions that I accompany him on a three day trip to a certain encampment pitched for the express purpose of pleasure, but succeeded in insisting that I had immediate business to attend to. What I had need of most, I said, was a small strong building where I could be certain of interviewing men without interruption. He appeared to understand perfectly what I meant and offered me the use of a little structure which he had had built to house a mad relative, now deceased. Less than two hours after my arrival in Ghardaia, therefore, I was in possession of a strong little pavilion in which to build my 'operating theatre.'

The operating theatre is an important part of the prison. It consists of a slab of one sort or another with leather manacles attached, a white cloth with a few old bloodstains, one strong arc-light, a select set of surgical instruments, and a bottle of chloroform. Four hours after I arrived in Ghardaia, my operating table was ready, the arc-light above it, the blood-stained sheet over it, the chloroform and instruments beside it, and I surveyed it with satisfaction.

Then, locking the door of the little pavilion behind me, I made my way to the Sun Bar, where, according to Freddie, Abdelkader ben Tahar was last seen.

My first sight as I opened the door was of a pale coffee-colored breast with a nipple like a ripe raisin. A man had just torn away part of the bodice of a young woman whom he now struck over the face

157

with a whip. The rest of the clients of the Sun Bar
smoked on without raising their eyelids. I walked as
discreetly as possible to the other end of the bar and
ordered mint tea. My accent over those few words
was evidently good enough not to arouse suspicion
that a white man was in their midst.

Soon the man left off whipping the girl, dashed her to
the floor, and strode outside into the street. The girl
lay breathless on the floor, her dress now in tatters
and her breasts and belly visible down to her navel.
She was still ignored by the various groups of Arabs
who were dotted about here and there in the smoky
room. At that point she looked up and saw me looking at her. She smiled ingratiatingly, limped to her
feet, and shuffled over to me, arranging the torn
cloth at her breasts. The men watched her without
interest, but now their eyes picked me out and briefly
questioned (without suspecting) my presence. I
cursed my bad luck. If I spoke to the girl, the rest of
the men, all attention now, would penetrate my dis-
guise, and, while I was not particularly afraid of
immediate hostility, I did not want it known that
there was a white man masquerading as an Arab in
Ghardaia. I made up my mind in a split second. As
the girl sidled up to me, I raised my arm and struck
her hard with the back of the hand across the mouth.
She reeled backwards again, spitting curses at me.
The rest of the company burst out laughing. I seized
my opportunity by following up the girl, striking at
her again and again amidst increasing laughter, until
she toppled backwards out into the street.
    In a moment I had clapped down a coin for my tea
on the counter and followed her through the bead
curtain. She was standing outside, screaming and
swearing in Arabic at the top of her voice. I

approached her, and, as she was about to scream, waved a handful of notes in front of her. Immediately, her anger left her. She began to fawn again. I took her by the arm and walked her down the street. I did not attempt to speak until she was safely installed in one of the rooms of my prison, for there was no question of restoring her liberty to her until Helen Seferis was safe. I couldn't risk its getting known that I had arrived; especially in the wake of the attempt to murder me on the way to Ghardaia.

When I spoke, I spoke in French.

She was hesitant, but she understood.

I had asked her to describe Abdelkader ben Tahar to me.

She answered me in a torrent of Arab curses and pigeon French, and after she had spoken to me for about a minute it occurred to me that Abdelkader ben Tahar was the man who had wielded the whip. This did not surprise me particularly. He was a pimp after all, frequented the Sun Bar, and she was probably one of his prostitutes. Her name was Aisha.

As I was giving her money, she grinned from ear to ear and let fall the torn flap of her dress. Her pale brown breasts with their interesting almond-shaped nipples were thus exposed. A moment later, I felt my head pulled down into their warmth. She was an exceedingly seasoned lay, with sex-lips as tough as rhinoceros-hide, and a manner to match. But at the same time, there was something smooth about her, and she was well oiled between the legs.

I laid her back, and spread her thick thighs wide apart, and bent to taste the tough, seasoned hide of her cunt lips. They tasted like cunt, yet had a somewhat leathery feel to them—it was extraordinary to bury my face in her mound and feel that I was gamahuching a cow. And I don't mean it as an insult, for, although she demonstrated the wear and tear of many years in her trade, she was also an artful fuck who knew how to use her body as an instrument of pleasure.

The snatch-hole between her legs was one that had been entered who knows how many times and by how many men, and yet when I took off my clothes and mounted her, my cock poised at the portal of her pussy, I somehow felt that I was her first and only; a good prostitute will make you feel that way.

She grabbed hold of my sword and pulled me to her by its head, and bringing me to the brink of her opening, proceeded to push me into her slash without skipping a beat.

The feel of the big, dark hand pressing my cock into the leathery skinned cunt created an extra element of excitement and swelling, and I could feel the head beginning to throb madly as I moved, rhythmically now, in and out of her insides.

She thrusted up to greet me in such a way that I felt embraced, held by her huge, wide hips. And in the course of our fucking, as I began to drive wildly into the gash between her legs, she would lift me into the cradle of those loins into a horizontal, midair position; her ass lifted from beneath her, her ankles and thighs holding the weight of us both.

This gave me a delicious entrance to her cunt, an access to the depth of her; thus, I simply buried my cock in her. Simultaneously, I sucked on those almond shaped nipples, pulling one into the depths of my mouth, then the other, and squeezing and molding each tit as I did.

She reached around and grabbed my buttocks and squeezed gently as I plowed her, pulling me to her, and pushing me deeper inside her. She was still holding me upward now, lifted slightly in the air in the leg cradles, and her cunt was like a tunnel to be entered by my train.

It was amazing, to my mind, that I could feel so devoted to every woman I fucked in the moment I was fucking her, and that this prostitute, this stranger who was indeed my "welcoming committee" in Ghardaia, was all that mattered in this moment of passion.

She squeezed my buttocks harder, pulled me in closer, and smashed her hips against my groin, pressing the leathery pussy into me as I pressed into her. This was the start of my orgasm, and she knew it, and from the moment it began its gurgle of sex fire in my groin until the semen spat out of my cock like a sudden burst of rain, she moved her cunt, her hips, her belly beneath me in a grasp of pleasurable contortions that made my coming a wild explosion of lust. I burst deep inside her womb. My cock was buried to the hilt, and she graciously accepted my seed, wanted it, pressed her pussy receptacle up to receive it.

In those last minutes, as the jism drained from the core of me and dribbled into her, I felt myself swept off into a tornado of lust, whereupon I fucked, and pummeled and pressed out the last of my juices.

I folded like a jackknife about her loins and then our bellies struck, quivered and liquefied in a welter of flesh and hairs. I rose from her reluctantly and looked down on the glistening mess of her sex. The dark hairs of her powerful mound rose upwards in writhing cattails above and around the broad pink weal, apparently the result of the pimp's whipping in the bar. She giggled as if it were something she was quite used to. It saddened me to see someone used to that kind of abuse. I raised her in my arms and carried her over to the bed. She smothered my face in kisses as I did so. Then I kissed her lips, for the first

161

time and I kissed her for a long time on the mouth before I finally left her, locked in the room.

I returned at once to the street in which the bar was located and sat against a wall in the shade and pretended to fall asleep. I had been in that position for about an hour when I saw my man approaching down the street. He was wearing the same clothes, an ordinary white burnoose over rather flashily-colored clothes with very elaborate riding boots. It struck me that his trade must prosper.

As he was passing me, I stood up behind him and prodded my gun in his ribs.

"Walk," I said. "I'll follow."

He did so without hesitation.

In that way, about an hour and a half after I had left Aisha, I returned with her pimp.

My first act on introducing him into the room where she lay naked on the bed was to give him a rabbit punch to the back of his neck. As he fell on his knees, my boot slammed home to his spine. He fell headlong with a groan on his face.

Aisha burst into hysterical laughter and there in front of me, and before I had time to realize what she was about to do, she bent over the pimp and spat on his face.

Ben Tahar groaned as he wiped the offending liquid from his eyes. He tried to make a grab for one of her ankles but she skipped nimbly out of the way. Then he remembered me. He looked up quickly and bared his teeth in hatred. He was crouching like an animal with his belly on the floor.

I lunged forward with my boot and struck him on the bridge of his nose. He squealed in pain and fell backwards again to the floor.

Aisha pummeled the bed with delight. She was

lying face downward on it, her plump buttocks trembling, her coarse voice concocting an indecipherable series of curses which she threw at his bashed-in head.

I watched for a moment and then I sat down on a chair and lit a cigarette.

"Give him some brandy," I said to her.

She shot me a look almost of dislike.

I repeated my order.

This time she hesitated and then obediently poured out a shot of cognac which she carried across to him.

My prisoner dashed it aside with the flat of his arm.

"Pour me one then," I said calmly.

She was grinning as she repeated her performance, this time carrying the drink over to me. I slapped her playfully on the bottom, swigged down my drink, and turned again to face the prostrate Arab.

"I'm going to give you two minutes to tell me where you found the diary of Helen Seferis," I said. "If you haven't told me in that time, I'm going to cut off one of your ears."

He looked at me with fear and hatred but he did not reply.

I watched the second hand of my watch tick out two minutes.

"Where did you find the diary?"

There was no reply.

I stood up, crossed the room towards him and dragged him across the floor into the next room. That room was the 'operating theatre'. I had him strapped to the slab before he realized what I was doing. A punch to his crotch settled the last kicking leg. I opened my cabinet of instruments and selected a medium scalpel. I put a little water on to boil over an alcohol burner, and stood back to view my patient.

The sweat was collecting on his forehead.

I switched on the arc-light and measured the chloroform in the bottle.

He watched me in horror.

It was when I tilted the lip of the bottle to a fluff of cotton-wool that his voice broke hoarsely out of his chest.

"It was in Temassine!"

I drew out my map and consulted it.

"You're lying," I said coldly.

"No! It was Temassine, I swear!"

I noticed that Aisha was standing unperturbed in the doorway. When she saw me looking at her she grinned. I returned to my victim.

"Helen Seferis was at least two weeks on a camel train. How do you explain that?"

He blinked in relief.

"It was two camel trains!" he said. "They met! She was sold from one to the other!"

"Good! Where is she now?"

"I don't know! I swear!"

"Tell me everything, from the very beginning, quickly!"

He began eagerly.

He met Helen Seferis in a brothel in Temassine, he said. He visited her three nights in succession and one night he found her diary. He couldn't read it but he thought it might be amusing so he took it away with him. She fought him for it but he knocked her senseless on the bed. Then, before he had the opportunity of having it translated, he had been arrested on suspicion of theft and the manuscript had fallen into the hands of the police.

"Who paid you to keep your mouth shut?"

"No one!"

"You're lying!"

He didn't reply.

I dropped the scalpel into the boiling water and watched it simmer. Then I again reached for the chloroform bottle.

This time he waited until the cotton wool was actually under his nose. He screamed out then that it was Poilu that ordered him not to tell. He promised to pin murder on him if he did. It was after the murder of the Sheikh. Up till that time Poilu wasn't particularly interested whether or not Helen Seferis was found. I asked him why not. He said he thought it was because Poilu didn't want to offend the Sheikh's sister by prosecuting a case against her brother.

I risked a shot in the dark.

"Who sent you to bring her back to Ghardaia?" I snapped.

His jaw dropped in surprise and then he replied without further hesitation:

"It was Poilu! He said he would drop the other charge if I would go and buy her from the brothel and deliver her to him in Ghardaia."

"And you did that?"

"Yes."

"And they dropped the charges against you?"

He nodded.

"And where is she now?"

"I don't know!" he whined.

I sat down and puffed on my cigarette. My hunch had been correct. If, as I had suspected, Helen Seferis was in or near Ghardaia, someone must have brought her back from Temassine. By a bold guess, I had now established that ben Tahar had been released from prison for the express purpose of delivering Helen Seferis to Poilu. It had been a shot in the dark, but not quite without the use of sights, for ben Tahar, after all, was a known buyer and seller of women, and he alone had known the exact whereabouts of the abducted woman. It made sense that whoever required her presence in Ghardaia would employ ben Tahar to arrange it.

"How long ago did all this happen? When did you deliver the woman to Poilu?"

"About three weeks after the Sheikh was murdered. He paid me and that's the last I saw of her."

"Poilu!" I said, as much to myself as to him. But of course! Who was in a better position to carry out dirty work in the area in which he was resident Police Chief? Ben Tahar had confirmed Poilu's interest in Rirha bent Ali. It was not unlikely, therefore, that Poilu had obtained Helen for Rirha's brother, the new Sheikh. Something of that kind anyway, not forgetting for a moment the ambiguous presence of the Egyptian, Mr. Zarouk. It was probable, I concluded, that ben Tahar was telling the truth when he said he didn't know the present whereabouts of the missing woman. He was only a pimp, after all, and Poilu was not likely to confide in him. For this reason, I told ben Tahar that he had saved his ear. This brought a burst of disappointed protest from Aisha who had been standing naked all the while in the doorway. As she attempted to get hold of the scalpel herself to do God knows what damage to the petrified ben Tahar, I swatted her hard with my open hand on the rump. She cried out, her eyes flashing, and tried to beat me with her fists as I crushed her naked sex and breasts against my clothed front. But soon I found her mouth with my own and a moment later she relaxed like a child in my arms. There was something wildly primal that drew me to this tough, yet feminine, prostitute.

It was evening now, too late really to put into

action the next part of the plan which was already taking shape in my imagination. Over Aisha's naked shoulder I caught the eye of ben Tahar. He was looking at me with mute hatred. I decided that it would do him no harm to spend the night strapped to the operating slab. Passing one arm round under Aisha's superb buttocks, I lifted her into my arms and carried her into the bedroom.

Aisha giggled with delight. Her soft creviced underside was balanced pertly over my sex. Knees apart, with her hands upon them, she had squatted suddenly and deliciously in such a position as to enable her to impale her cunt upon my cock, which was in an agitated state of excitement. Contracting the muscles of her cunt, she came down on my cock like a cunt with soft claws, ready to squeeze me in.

A slight anticipatory trickle of sex juice appeared at her sex-lips and fell like a drop of spring rain on to my erection. With my hands under her hips I raised my erection until it brushed against the lips of her sex. In response, she raised herself slightly, and, uttering an inarticulate animal sound of triumph, pressed the opening of her cunt onto the head of my cock. She rubbed herself around it, until her pussy was ripe with warm, juicy wetness. The intimate feel of her hole mingling warmly with my prick caused me to leap upwards lustfully with my loins, bringing my hard male core in even more direct contact with her dripping mound. I struck and slid easily inward, her warm fleshy parts fitting over me like a muffler, her soft leathery outer parts fitting like a glove over my groin. As I made a hard bow of my torso, she rode me madly as a naked woman might ride a saddle-horn. Her long dark hair, meanwhile, fell in a blue-black veil over her face, breaking on her cheekbones, so that her eyes, like dark jewels, glinted ecstatically from amongst the hair, while her hands, steadying herself on my hips, bit into my flesh with long nails. My own hands were hypnotized by the smooth swell of her brown buttocks, caressing, teasing, testing the warm chubs of female flesh which alternatively sat and rose from my dripping thighs. Meanwhile, I watched her powerful mound at work. Cloven like a goat's foot, the brown and pink flesh shone through the wet black hairs in its terrible desire to crush itself against my member while, above it, her belly thrust itself forward, the muscles sucking my member deeply into the crevice of her cunt. She was breathing heavily, undulating from her ribcage downward on the axle that extended beneath the twisting flesh of her belly to the coarse-haired mound which nuzzled me. As I felt its pressure, rough, soft, and yielding at the same time, I felt my own urgency mounting upwards between my buttocks and coursing like a spiderweb of electricity at the soft mass beneath my member. I reached into the juicy mound of pussy flesh and, uncovering the hard, erect bud of her clitoris, began to rub it feverishly with my thumb, while she continued to pummel her flesh against mine.

At that moment, she howled like a Dervish and brought her hot and horny rump downward with all the force of her body onto the seeping triangle of short hairs which I raised to her. A pencil of blackness passed upwards through me and was followed immediately by a spark which crackled sinuously through the veins of my abdomen, and broke, taut and sleek, in a hot white eruption at my phallus. No sooner had I shuddered thus to my climax than, with another yell, she unsworded herself and brought her teeming loins to my mouth. The last twist of passion at my loins coincided with my receiving her hot and musky smelling cunt at my mouth.

I took the shivering mound of flesh into my mouth and licked deeply at the taut-skinned hole, feeling her press the swollen lips and folds into my face. Grabbing hold of the fleshy inner thighs, I pulled her closer yet, and as my tongue discovered the hard and bursting clit, I could feel the hot juice of desire beginning to drip from between the brown lips of her slash. I sucked the clit, simultaneously pulling at her flesh in such a way that it caused the bud of love to vibrate back and forth, and suddenly she pressed herself with all her might and began riding my mouth in frantic, pressing motions. All my attention went into the hard, measured sucking of her clit and the frenzied pace of her gyrating pussy let me know I was sucking her into a state of excitement where wave after wave of pleasure was washing through her cunt. The inner sanctum was twitching with a seizure of passion.

She grabbed my head and pulled my face closer in as she shook through the last of her creamy contractions. Finally, I felt the dewy emission of her sex trickle from her cunt to my lips. I lapped at the liquid, which clung to the outer folds of her cunt until at last, the swell of passion had subsided.

Chapter 7

I awoke quite early. Aisha's naked body was stretched out beside me, her large breasts visible above the sheet.

I climbed out of bed and washed and dressed quietly without waking her. I made some coffee and took a cup to ben Tahar who had spent an uncomfortable night on the slab. I freed his hands, allowed him to sit up, and watched him drink. When he had finished, I released his legs and ushered him at gunpoint down to the cellar where I pointed to a bunk.

"With luck," I said to him in French, "I'll be able to spring you in twenty-four hours."

He sat down on the bunk without replying. I locked the heavy door behind me as I left. Shortly afterwards, having locked the outside door to the prison, I made my way slowly through the quarter towards the center of the town.

As far as I could see, there was only one course open to me. It would be necessary to kidnap Colonel Poilu and to interview him in the intimacy of the operating theatre. At first sight, perhaps, this might have seemed more dangerous than a similar seizure of any of the others who appeared on the 'roll-call'. But in fact it was not so.

There were four remaining names on the list, that of the Sheikh, that of the Sheikh's sister, that of Zarouk, and that of my selected victim. To kidnap the Sheikh himself would have been an exceedingly dangerous operation. He would, I realized at once, be constantly surrounded by his bodyguard, especially in view of the fact that his brother had been assassinated so recently. As for the sister, the beautiful Rirha, I doubted whether I would be able to convince her that I would really go so far as to disfigure her if she didn't talk. I might have managed to abduct her but I was doubtful about the utility of doing so. And, as far as Zarouk was concerned, I didn't even know his present whereabouts.

The following information I had derived from my good source, Aisha:

The Sheikh lived in his palace not far from the centre of the town, and his sister, often as not, was with him. Poilu had his official residence in the center of the town, although it was rumored that he spent most of his time in a smart modern flat which the Sheikh's sister sometimes occupied in the main street. He was, that is to say, easy to contact in his daily journeys between the fort, the official residence, and the "fuck flat" of his mistress. Zarouk from beginning to end was more elusive than the rest; he might be anywhere between Cairo and Tangiers. Of him, except that she had seen him once or twice in the company of Poilu, Aisha knew nothing.

I had seen men like Zarouk in many North African cities. They are the men most difficult to get at, the men for whom crimes are committed but who are never themselves brought to trial. They have their paid men everywhere. They know when to get out of a hot situation and leave the minions to take the rap. And I'd had an uncanny feeling for the past few days that it was with Zarouk that I would finally have to settle.

Again, all evidence up to date confirmed my impression that it was Colonel Poilu himself who knew what I wanted to know. Helen Seferis was brought to Ghardaia on his instructions and for reasons best known to himself: he had neither consulted nor informed the police authorities in Algiers, and they, if they suspected anything, preferred to keep quiet about it. Colonel Poilu, then, was probably quite au courant with all information pertaining to the whereabouts, past and present, of Helen Seferis, while, as far as the other three were concerned, and while I guessed that they knew everything, I could not be quite sure. Thus the colonel himself was the next logical victim.

To kidnap the resident Chief of Police might sound a bold undertaking, but one should never allow oneself to be impressed by externals. When I considered the matter calmly, I came to the conclusion that there would be less risk in kidnapping him than in the abduction of any of the other three. A police chief, after all, must derive a very real sense of security from his position. In a well-ordered town like Ghardaia, it was unlikely that he would feel any sense of personal risk, especially in view of the fact that he was on such intimate terms with the reigning

Sheikh. And, once in my prison, there would be little risk of his causing me further embarrassment, for, if things went as I expected, he would be in no position to prosecute me when the affair was over.

It was a beautiful morning when I issued from my headquarters in the tent-scattered suburbs of the town and I made my way without hesitation to the main street in which the few first class hotels as well as the private apartment of Rirha bent Ali was situated. It was in that quarter that the European element congregated and passed their days of exile.

Exile. The word made me think of London where Laura was. It occurred to me that she would be opening the office about this time. The thought that she might have given herself during the night to another man made me inexplicably jealous. Her thighs crowned by pubic hair of dark auburn were some of the most beautiful I had ever seen. That made me wonder why I hadn't married her, taken a cottage somewhere by the sea, and spent the rest of my life venting my lust legally. But here I was in a hot Arab town, dressed like an Arab, shuffling like a leper closer to where two French officers were sipping cool drinks in a shady hotel garden. It occurred to me that I was a maniac. No woman, not even Laura herself, was worth all this physical discomfort.

I was close enough now to be able to see that neither of the officers held the rank of Colonel. One was a young subaltern and the other was a major, probably the very adjutant who had sent the Seferis document to Mr. Pamandari, Nadya's almost mythological father and the firm friend of the irascible Lord Grisskillin. The thought of Grisskillin made me smile. I had never earned an easier thousand pounds than those he paid me to look after Nadya.

I shuffled on until I was opposite the smart apartment building in which the amorous life of the Sheikh's sister was carried on without obvious issue. I thought that it would be regretful if I were forced to leave Ghardaia without first tasting her charms. My impression up to date had been that if I had been on the other side she would not have been adverse to my advances. I was daydreaming in this way when an old but highly polished Rolls Royce came to a majestic halt outside the apartment building.

I immediately recognized the man who stepped from it as the French officer who had sat with Rirha bent Ali in Le Bosphore on the night when Rosemary Dalton was kidnapped. He was in uniform and I saw at once that he held the rank of colonel. I concluded that this was my prey.

Poilu walked straight into the apartment building, leaving the Arab chauffeur seated at the wheel. I walked closer to get a better view of the man who sat in the car. He was roughly my own age, unbearded like myself and wore a red fez. I glanced along the street. It was almost deserted. I had already decided to change places with him.

Affecting an air of insolence I walked across the road and looked in at the monkey through the windscreen. He glared out angrily at me. Without hesitation I began then to unscrew the silver mascot from off the radiator. He looked at me with a dumbfounded expression on his face for about ten seconds and then, opening the front door violently, he stepped out to confront me. As he reached forward to grab me, I stuck my Mauser brutally into his belly.

"Quick!" I said. "Walk in front of me into the building!"

He began to back away but when he saw my hand clench around the gun he turned suddenly and walked meekly in front of me into the building. The concierge, fortunately, was not in the hall. I made the man walk quickly in front of me through the hall and down a back stair which led to the cellars, and then as we were walking along a narrow passage I tipped off his fez and brought the butt of my automatic sharply against his right temple. He fell like a log. Without haste, I lifted him onto my shoulders and carried him through an opening into a kind of underground hall skirted on all sides by cellar doors with padlocks on them. I broke open one padlock with the butt of my automatic and carried the unconscious chauffeur through into the cellar where I dumped him unceremoniously on the concrete floor. I bound his hands and legs, gagged him, and left, putting the prong of the broken padlock through the hasp and arranging it as far as possible to look as though it hadn't been interfered with. In the passage I picked up and donned the fez and walked quickly upstairs into the upper hall. As I passed through it I saw through the glass doors that Colonel Poilu had already returned to the car. He was standing outside with his hand on one of the back door handles. I crept forward up to the doors and stood behind the glass watching to see what he would do. He seemed to be undecided and then, suddenly, he opened the rear door and leaned inside as though he were about to take something from the back seat.

In a split second I made up my mind. I thrust my way through the doors of the apartment house, walked quietly and quickly across the pavement, pushed Poilu into the car with my left hand, and gave him a sharp rabbit punch with the right. The back of the car was spacious. He toppled forward neatly onto the floor. I had only to lift in his ankles and feet and no one, I realized, would have suspected anything from the hotels along the street. I stepped backwards quickly and closed the door. Only one Arab walked slowly towards me along the street and I could see by the expression on his face that he suspected nothing. Swiftly I walked round the car, stepped into the driving seat, and drove off quietly along the road.

I turned one of the interior mirrors downward so that I could watch Poilu through the glass partition which divided the chauffeur from his employer. In that way I drove confidently through the town and right up to the door of my prison. The time was 10 a.m. I considered that things were moving very satisfactorily.

I walked Poilu at gunpoint from the car to the pavilion and, once inside, straight through into the operating theatre. Aisha, inquisitive and naked, followed.

In my grill room I strapped him immediately to the slab, or rather Aisha did—she had been cooperative from the beginning, and didn't appear to think it at all unnatural that I locked her in every time I went out—and, without listening to his pompous protests, walked straight out of the house again.

My object was to get rid of the car which was standing elegantly outside, as large as a flag for evidence. A crowd had already collected and one skinny child was attempting to screw the mascot off the radiator. I waded my way through them and drove quickly away. At a safe distance I again parked the car, removed my chauffeur's fez, and walked quickly back towards the pavilion. My return took about five minutes, five minutes that I hadn't wanted to waste. During the brief second when I took my decision and strode through the glass door to push Poilu into the car, I had not thought what I was going to do with the car. It was only as I drove through the streets and saw that the car's progress was watched from all sides by grinning street urchins that I realized that if I had advertised on the front page of the News of the World I could not have made the knowledge of my itinerary more universal. For that reason, I realized as I drove along that the exposure of my prison, should I drive right up to it, was certain within a space of hours, perhaps less. And yet there was nothing else to do. Of course, I could have stepped out of the car and deserted my victim far away from my hideout, but then the whole black band of them might very well have been alerted within half an hour and my whole plan of action would have been ruined. I had to go through with it now and that meant that instead of having all the time in the world to grill the colonel, I had, perhaps, less than was necessary. I cursed myself for a fool, but the harm was already done for I couldn't carry him through the streets in broad daylight nor, had I waited for him to come to, could I have walked him in broad daylight at the point of a gun. In spite of my burnoose, the attitudes of two men taking a walk of that nature through a busy town would have brought attention from passersby. That was why I decided to go through with it as I did, lose time as I parked the car away at a safe distance, and only then return to grill Poilu. Every minute was precious. I almost ran.

The crowd was still undispersed. I cursed my luck, put on an air of authority and passed in through to the house. I relocked the door on the inside. Then I made my way straight to the surgery room.

The first sight that greeted me as I entered was the colonel's bare belly, the sex rampant above it, and the serpent-like tongue of Aisha teasing the swollen mushroom at the end of the rubbery pipe. She'd been knelt over him like that for quite some time and, in the interim, she'd sucked his cock with great abandon, while putting her swollen pussy lips on his mouth. The Colonel licked his way into the soft leathery cunt lips, and he'd tongued the swollen clit to such a point that Aisha had come in his mouth. He then licked the juicy emissions away and sent her into a state of excitement again, momentarily gaining her favor as he rekindled the passion-fire that had somewhat faded after the first come.

She rode his face, pressed the pussy petal down on his tongue, rubbing the hardness of her clit against his lips, and pressing herself down to greet his sucking tongue.

He took the whole of the swollen clit bud in his mouth, and wrapped his lips around it like a tight ring, and squeezed at her sex until the beginnings of an explosion again began to rumble through her lower parts. He licked back and forth on it, flicked the bud this way and that as he pulled it into the grasp of his mouth, heightening her pleasure with sensations of squeezing, sucking, licking. And Aisha came once again into the Colonel's mouth.

She was returning the favor when I walked in. As she tongued his big cock with her wet mouth, I could still see the glimmer of her come on his chin. She grinned as I entered and, like the little bitch she was, pretended playfully to bite off the tip.

The colonel squealed like a pig and then, as she held her naked flanks in laughter, he turned towards me and said pompously:

"You'll hang for this!"

I had no time to waste. I walked over to him and broke his nose with a blow of my fist. The blood bubbled upwards and spilled over his chin onto his uniform, the first blood, I suppose, which had ever spilled over that particular uniform. Then, quickly, I filled a basin full of cold water, took a handful of cotton wool, and passed both things over to Aisha.

"Bathe his nose," I said, and, to the colonel: "While she does that, keep your ears open, Poilu! I'm going to tell you what I want from you and I'm going to tell you what's going to happen to you if I don't get it. Do you understand?"

He moaned.

"Listen carefully," I continued. "I want to know where Helen Seferis is, if you've got her yourself or if you passed her on after ben Tahar delivered her to you. Have you got that? Where is Helen Seferis? Next, what'll happen to you if you don't come across. Understand? Aisha here is going to bite you off…Aisha…is…going…to…bite…you…off…!"

I moved up to his head, took over from Aisha and pointed to his loins. With a giggle, she returned to her game, bent over his cock, sucking it now in a menacing way.

"Where is Helen Seferis?"

He made to speak but fell silent, hatred in his eyes.

I signalled to Aisha. She applied gentle pressure, still sucking, she now gnawed ever-so-slightly on the still-hard rubbery rod. A look of astonished horror crossed his face. His erection was gone.

"Where is Helen Seferis?"

Again he made to speak. Aisha applied more pressure, but then suddenly I saw a fathead stubbornness grow in his rather handsome colorless eyes, and it occurred to me that I had spoilt his looks before I even got a good look at them. For a moment our eyes met. He must have noticed uncertainty in mine, for a moment later a look of stubborn certainty came into his. I realized that he had called my bluff. I had been a fool not to go through with my original plan with the chloroform. I would have donned my surgeon's gloves, selected my scalpel, and have threatened to remove his left eye. If he hadn't talked, I would have removed the eye from the socket, temporarily, by a little surgical trick, removing the vision, and then continued with a threat to the right eye. He wouldn't have been able to talk fast enough.

But now this plan didn't appear to be so sound. He certainly wouldn't have talked before I had removed the first eye and, with the threat of pursuit growing every minute, I was in no mood for such an operation. For a moment I thought I had lost. It was then that his deflated sex gave me an idea.

Quickly I tipped up the slab to an angle of forty-five degrees, at the same time baring his pubic region completely. Then I placed a mirror so that he could see himself. Next, I made a long needle red hot and placed it horizontally over his member, securing it in position by means of a surgical frame.

"And now, Poilu, start talking!" I said. "Aisha is going to excite you and I'm not going to interfere. If you don't tell, you're going to lose it after all. You're going to have to control it yourself."

The sweat was standing out on his brow as Aisha came near his head with her great thighs. She began to tickle his lips with her short hairs, squatting over the slab to do it. I lit a cigarette and sat back. What a beautiful muscled mound Aisha had…she, like the dancer in the village I stayed in, would have been a valuable addition to my merry company in London! I turned my eyes downward to watch his reaction. Slowly, very slowly, his member redressed itself. It was a fantastic sight. At one end, rigid under the naughty buttocks of Aisha, his face was seized in a grimace of fear, the perspiration gathering at his temples, while, at the other, in spite of his determination, his passion gathered itself towards the needle like paper curling towards a hot fire. I prepared myself.

At the moment at which he screamed, I removed the frame and shot the question at him again.

"Where is Helen Seferis!"

"She's here, in Ghardaia!" he gasped.

"Where?"

"She's in the palace, you fool! You'll never find her! You'll hang for this! I'll have you burned alive!"

Aisha, true to her vocation, began to touch herself, rubbing her titties, running her fingers through her mound and masturbating her swelling clit. At the same time, Poilu let out a noise like a punctured tyre which ended, as such a noise sometimes does, with a kind of whinnying raspberry.

I hesitated only a moment longer. For all the good it did me, I had my information, or as much, anyway, as I had time to force from this reactionary police chief. To wait longer in my hideout would be dangerous. I could still hear the noise of the crowd outside. I considered that it was time to disappear and prepare my last move. The move now would be fraught with all kinds of dangers. My enemies would be aware of everything as soon as Poilu was discovered. There was only one thing to do: that was to put the remainder of my plan into operation without delay. I would have to go immediately to the palace and risk everything in a last frantic bid to contact the missing woman. To tell the truth, I knew very well that I had lost control of the situation. My chances of survival, far less of success, had decreased almost to nil. Nevertheless, I took care to chloroform Poilu before I left the operating theatre. The longer he remained out of commission, the better. As for Aisha, I told her that things were looking very black, that she had better consider her own future before she made any further move. She wanted to accompany me. I'm sure she would have done anything in her power to help me. But there was little she could do. She herself would be in great danger as soon as ben Tahar was free. I advised her to go as quickly as possible to the house of 'Hadj' Mohan ben Abdelahman and to ask him, as a last favor to me, to protect her. I kissed her then for the last time and walked through the intervening room towards the exit.

At that moment, the door opened inward and I stopped short. It was Rirha bent Ali. She had a gun in her hand and she was pointing it at me.

Chapter 8

"You're just in time for lunch!" I said with heavy irony, watching with impotence the four Arabs who entered the room behind her. Each was armed to the teeth. There was no possibility of escape.

The sphinx didn't even bother replying. She made a sign to her henchmen who closed in about me, secured my wrists and walked me out through the door into the street. Outside, there was no sign of the police. I was hustled through the crowd and driven away in a black car with blinds drawn.

A few minutes later I was prodded roughly across a small courtyard and down into a cellar. There I was thrown into a corner on a heap of straw and the heavy door was closed and bolted behind me.

In a space of minutes the tables had been turned. There was little doubt in my mind that I had reached the end of a short happy life. They had disarmed me in the car but they had left my cigarettes. I smoked one now, thinking that soon Colonel Poilu would appear. That worried me. I could expect short shrift at the hands of the man I had so recently humiliated. I had an uneasy thought that he looked like the kind of man who would not lack imagination in devising a slow death. The thought of suicide crossed my mind, but at an academic level only. I rejected it immediately, not because I placed any intellectual trust in the maxim that while there is life there is hope, but because, at a biological level, I was the victim of a kind of pathetic constipation; I was unable, as it were, to pass the turd of self-annihilation.

There was little light in the dungeon and I was not comforted by what I saw when I struck the match to light my cigarette. A dead man dangled from a set of wall chains, his back towards me. The skin of his back had been cut to shreds by some kind of whip and his lifeless head dangled from his shoulders like a turnip on string. I blew out my match thoughtfully. I was not inquisitive about the corpse and felt no urge to examine it more closely. The odor of death mingled with my tobacco smoke.

I sat smoking and thinking for more than two hours. I was not wracking my brains for a plan of escape. Only a fiction detective does that kind of thing. The professional assumes that there is no possibility of escape until a piece of direct contrary evidence asserts itself. Sitting in a stone dungeon with no knowledge of the power and intentions of your captor, and with the suspicion that both are extreme, you are in no position to frame even the most general plan of escape. To do so is not only to waste time but to increase your nervous tension. The most effective thing to do is to meditate until such time as your intelligence has more data to work upon.

When my captors finally came, there was again no question of escape—four guards who cuffed my hands behind my back this time and walked me through a series of complicated passages to a huge cellar illuminated by burning torches and in the center of which stood a gallows and a dangling rope. When my feet hesitated, my jailors thrust me forward roughly to the foot of the scaffold.

Only one thing was out of key. For an audience, instead of a ring of grim-faced men, was the most luxuriant assortment of naked women, of every race, black, brown, yellow, and white, their beefy or sinuous flesh oiled and gleaming in the flickering torches. There was something prehistoric—an ambiguous symptom of an archaic race—in the shadowy lunges of their naked torsos, their round bellies, below which hair knotted at the gnarl of their thighs like a tree trunk in which rough dry grass thrust itself outward obstinately. Their breasts too had a kind of lean tigerish suggestion, and their smell, encouraged from their warm female limbs by the heavy fire-lit atmosphere, wafted to my nostrils. When their mouths opened, the whiteness of teeth flashed. Above, on the firelit roof, the magnified shadows seethed slickly about like a warm sexual blood of a virgin's soft, rended skin. It was overpowering, the dead stalk of the gallows itself, with its massive hawser-like rope, surrounded by the thick naked thighs, thrust-haired mounds, ankles and naked feet. My captors thrusting upwards from behind, lifted me into the noose.

At the moment at which they opened the trapdoor I felt my hands cut free from behind, and I found myself swinging in the heavy collar, the leash of which I grasped and pulled upwards on with both hands. As I swung about like a plumb-line, my toes pointing long pencils of shadow across the sea of women's breasts, I became aware that a woman was standing on the dais beside me and that in her hand she carried a black raw-hide whip. It was Rirha bent Ali.

Her beautiful body was quite naked except for the barbaric jewelry she wore at her wrists and ankles. She was smiling at me almost lazily.

"You did not take my warning, Meester 'Arvest!"

I had no sooner heard the words when the first terrible cut of the whip struck through the cloth of my shirt and seared my skin. I heard her laugh softly, and, as I opened my eyes, saw her face in front of me. There was little expression on it, a slight smile at the corner of the lips, a tinge of humor in the eyes. I tried to smile disdainfully but it was difficult with two inches of tongue jammed between my teeth by the pressure of the rope at my neck. In another moment, unless I exerted my arms more, I was going to swallow it and suffocate.

"How foolish a man you must be!" I heard her voice come again, "Do you not realize that you have no friend in this part of the country? Poilu and I are the law of this country. You had the audacity to come and interfere with us!"

No sooner had the whip landed this time than I felt her fingers tearing the clothes off my body. Sometimes her long nails slashed at my flesh as she rended the material apart. A moment later, I was hanging stark naked before the grinning women and I was aware that my member, excited in some subterranean way by this death-dance, had increased to an enormous size and stuck upwards like a tree out of my lower belly. Suddenly it was seized by one of the women who applied her thick lips to it and pulled downward on my body at the same time so that if I had not exerted the full force of my arms on the rope above I would have been strangled. I remembered at that moment that a man is supposed to experience his greatest orgasm at the moment when he is hanged. Ah, *Le Petit Mort*! The thought of it made my beet rise all the harder into the big suckling mouth of the Negress who crouched before me, her big breasts against my shins and one of her thumbs thrust cruelly in my centerpiece. Nevertheless, my arms refused to assist in my execution and clung like steel bands to the throttling rope above my head. And I dangled there as the woman lavished long wet licks and deep warm sucks on my rampant rod, awed that I was receiving such deliciously dangerous sexual tortures.

I became aware again of Rirha's voice:

"If you had taken my advice," she said, "your Helen Seferis would have soon been at liberty. Now there is no chance, and I am quite certain that you are not fool enough still to be hoping for yourself!"

The third cut came. It was followed quickly and regularly be six further cuts, and, at the stroke of the sixth, I felt a hot skin of blood rise and move like a glass blade over the tender flesh of my back to the tight muscles of my straining buttocks.

I nearly lost consciousness. I felt a sudden ridiculous impulse to protest. It rose along my tongue and was stifled painfully at the strong vice of my teeth. Tears were running from my eyes and the room with its cargo of female flesh and sweat turned like a tub in a whirlpool, causing a razor of pain at my temples. I was breathing hoarsely through my nose, and I felt the sweat running from my face onto my chest and trickling like a terrible itch towards the hairs of my groin where the black woman brayed and spat her terrible lust at my member.

She had my balls cupped in one hand, my cock in

the other, and as she pressed her lips upon my hard organ, and rode her mouth up and down the length of my cock, she was rocking the come right out of me by squeezing my cock at it's base, and running her fisted brown fingers up and down the length of the lower part of my rod. At some moments, she'd flick intensely at the head, and lick the sensitive skin between the head and shaft, and drive me into an ecstasy that was uncontrollable in any position—and deadly in the position I was in.

She was sucking me, and I was fighting off the choking at my neck, wanting to succumb to the pleasure, and being strangely, obscenely tantalized at knowing succumbing to the pleasure could mean turning myself over to death, as well.

The whip was rising and falling relentlessly and I came to know it only as a knifeblade at my inmost nerve. I felt my wrists crumble away like sand from the rope that was hanging me, and my fingers were grazed as they strove feebly to bite into the hard hemp. At that moment, my lower belly was riven with ecstasy and all feeling seemed to merge with a hungry slobber of lust.

The woman at my groin sucked and pummeled at my cock until the wild, uncontained expression of my sex came rushing through me like a tidal wave of unstoppable pleasure. She held my manhood firmly as the raging torrent of jism splashed through me like a fiery volcano and into her warm, wet, inticing mouth.

Chapter 9

One comes back to consciousness via a different road, thrusting upwards, contained within a second circle of frowning walls. And then suddenly it is light, and your eyes hurt and there is water under clenched lids. And this time there was the thick ache at my neck and the vicious needling sensation at my back. I must have groaned.

The woman walked closer to me. It occurred to me that I was dreaming, or maybe I was dead and this was heaven, for I was looking up at the most beautiful woman that I had ever seen in my life. She wore a dove-grey peignoir of fine velvet over the sleek lines of her body, the material rising sheerly upwards above her breasts to a stiff collar, high, and almost touching the superb chin. The long almond-shaped eyes were even more grey than the velvet, grey, tinged with amethyst beneath the bold line of her eyebrows, which were raised, speculatively at the idiocy of my expression. Her platinum-blonde hair fell softly from her temples over her shoulders and halfway down her back. She leaned forward and placed a lit cigarette in my mouth. My lips closed over it mechanically and I inhaled deeply.

She spoke a moment later.

"You were looking for me?"

It crossed my mind to say I had been looking for her all my life but the words melted in my mouth and I said nothing.

She smiled and lit a cigarette for herself. I watched every movement, fascinated by her grace. And then she looked at me again, blowing flame and smoke away from the tip of the match and allowing it to fall to the floor from between her tapering fingers.

"I am Helen Seferis," she said softly. "I hear I owe you my freedom."

I closed my eyes with a groan. The memories came flooding back—Poilu on the operating table, Rirha bent Ali smiling at me as I hanged, the sudden terrible ecstasy at my vitals before I lost consciousness. I was under a hallucination. Reality fled away from me. I screwed my eyes tightly in their sockets. And then, with my hand shading them, I allowed them gradually to flicker open.

The woman was still there! She was smiling at my consternation, such a smile and with such superbly full lips as I had never seen on any woman. I breathed heavily, my eyes fixed on this goddess who smiled tenderly at my madness. My senses began to swim and then her hand was moving toward my forehead slowly, until it touched, cool as the long fingers massaged the beginning of my scalp and the knot of pain between my eyebrows.

"You are quite handsome," she said smiling down at me. "Does your head hurt?"

I shook my head helplessly.

"I owe you more than I can say," she said.

I spoke at last. "You're free?"

"Of course! Can't you see I am?"

"I don't understand," I said. "I can't remember anything after they hanged me...till now, I mean, everything is black."

"Don't worry about it just now," she said softly. "Try to sleep. Later, you will take me to London. I have never been to London."

My eyelids were heavy. They drooped. I must have lost consciousness again.

It was evening when I woke. I was lying in the same white-walled room, the bed soft, rich carpets strewn about the floor. Outside, I could see the stars glimmering in the sky and the white wall of some building or other almost phosphorescent in the moonlight. Vaguely, I heard voices in the court outside. I closed my eyes, reopened them, and raised one hand to my neck. There was a bandage on it. Beneath the bandage it felt thick and sore. The pain in my back had diminished. I felt almost as though I could get up. Soon I made out the shape of a candle and candlestick which stood on a brass table by the side of the bed. I reached out my hand and touched it. The back of my hand touched brass and then suddenly the shape of a matchbox. I grasped it, took out a match and struck it. It spurted into flame, making a lantern within my hands. I lit the candle.

Then the memory of Helen Seferis came back to me. Had I been dreaming? She had said I had saved her. How? Had I died and come back? A thousand uncomfortable questions swam about in my head. I

heard the sound of a cart turning in the court outside.
I centered my thoughts about it, heard a man's voice
shout something in Arabic, and then the noise of the
wheels again. I was suddenly aware of the packet of
English cigarettes beside the long candlestick. I took
it and lit one. What had happened. Poilu? Zarouk?
And Rirha bent Ali? I felt I must be going mad.
Then, suddenly, there was a discreet knock on the
door and an Arab girl appeared through the bead
curtains. She carried a plate with a letter on it. When
she saw I was awake, she walked across to the bed
and held the plate towards me. I smiled at her but
her face remained expressionless. She nodded
towards the letter. I accepted it and immediately she
turned and left the room as silently as she had come.

I raised the letter to my nostrils. It was scented
subtly with a female's perfume. Turning round in the
bed, I held it beneath the candle and opened it with
my forefinger. I drew out the following letter:

Dear Mr. Harvest,

*I hope you have quite recovered from the rough
treatment that was accorded you. In a sense, it was
your own fault. It was really an intrepid, not to say
foolish undertaking to run directly against the combined power of the French Resident and the local
Arab authority. How could you have hoped to succeed? And, if you had found Helen Seferis, how could
you have escaped from Algeria with her? You should
consider yourself very lucky to be alive and free.
However, in a sense, we—my brother, Sheikh Hussein
and myself—are indebted to you, to you and to the
girl you left to look after Colonel Poilu. I shall explain
as shortly as I can.*

*A month before my late brother was assassinated at
Laghouat, Hussein, my living brother who is the present Sheikh, made a deal with Colonel Poilu. My late
brother and Poilu were not on friendly terms, not*

194

politically, personally, I mean. Poilu hinted to Hussein that if the Sheikh was murdered they would pin it on some fanatic. Hussein agreed to get rid of my eldest brother if Poilu guaranteed to see that nothing came in the way of Hussein becoming Sheikh. I knew nothing of all this although I knew that Poilu hated my late brother.

One of the reasons was myself. Poilu wanted me to marry him and my brother refused to allow it. I suppose that Poilu hoped Hussein would make me marry him. Hussein was foolish enough to confirm the plan in a letter. Then, suddenly, two days before Hussein's plan was carried into operation, the Sheikh was murdered at Laghouat. Hussein was jubilant. I accused him of being responsible for the murder. He laughed and said it was true he had planned to murder our brother but that Allah had been kind enough to do it for him.

That might have been all. But Poilu had a friend—your good friend Zarouk! Zarouk is a kind of international gambler; he is wanted for a capital offense in Egypt. The Egyptian government asked the late Sheikh to extradite him. He agreed. That was perhaps the strongest reason for which Poilu wanted my brother out of the way. In the face of the Egyptian request, the French government would never have condoned Poilu's prohibiting my brother from doing his duty. But Hussein had guaranteed to refuse the Egyptian request. That brings us to the assassination.

Hussein had nothing to do with that. But he could not prove it, and Poilu had the letter in which Hussein confirmed his intention to arrange for the assassination. Therefore, as soon as the Sheikh was murdered, Poilu had Hussein at his mercy. He let it be known that unless Hussein did just as he was told, he, Poilu, would arrest him in the name of the the French government on a charge of fratricide. He would produce the letter and arrange for the assassination of Hussein before he came to trial. Meanwhile, he made no effort to track down the real criminal.

Hussein agreed to do as he was told. The first thing that Poilu wanted was to marry me. I refused. Hussein had me taken to him. Poilu used me. He said he was going to go on using me but that now he had no intention of marrying me. Poilu seemed to go mad. His demands were impossible. The man behind him was Zarouk. Zarouk had the ideas and Poilu had the power. Now, as you know, the Helen Seferis manuscript had come before Poilu. He didn't care himself one way or the other, but Hussein asked him not to compromise the family by forcing the Arab who found the manuscript to speak. Then Zarouk saw the manuscript and he immediately wanted Helen Seferis to be found for his own use. Poilu never refused him anything. He released the Arab, ben Tahar, to go and bring her to Ghardaia. He did so.

That was the position before you came on the scene. Poilu and Zarouk wanted to get rid of you at once. They would have done so. But it was my agent who trapped you on the train and he had explicit instructions not to kill you. I think I thought even at the time that you might be useful to me.

Meanwhile, Hussein and I had decided that we had taken enough from Poilu. We would have to arrange to have him put out of the way. But Hussein was afraid of the consequences. We hesitated too long. Poilu got the wind of it. He came to see me on the morning you kidnapped him and told me that he intended to have Hussein assassinated and to produce the letter. That would mean that my youngest brother, a mere boy of twelve, would have become the titular Sheikh. Poilu then would be in complete control. Hussein, he said, would be arrested within fifteen minutes of his leaving me. He would 'resist' arrest and be shot trying to escape. Fortunately, Mr. Harvest, he had not reckoned he'd have to deal with you. He never had the opportunity to arrest Hussein. At the precise moment when everything seemed lost, you stepped in and removed Poilu.

As you can imagine, I had to act quickly. There was

no time for second thoughts. You were removed
quickly because you would only have complicated
explanations. The subsequent treatment that was
accorded you had nothing to do with the main
story—a little game of my own, and you will have to
believe me when I say that no harm was intended!
Meanwhile, there was Poilu. That was arranged very
neatly. He was forced to make love to Aisha at gunpoint, and then, when he was beginning to enjoy himself, he was dispatched forthwith. Ben Tahar, who
turns out to be Aisha's legal husband will be tried for
his murder, but with the laws as they are, he will probably get off with a brief sentence or a fine. After all, he
caught his wife and her lover in flagrant delicto. He
will be well paid to stick to his story. The compromising letter was found in Poilu's wallet and destroyed.

As for Zarouk, as soon as he heard of the death of
his protector, he disappeared completely. I hope sincerely that we have heard the last of him. Helen Seferis
was found locked in one of the upstairs rooms in his
house.

I am happy to say that everything appears to be
about to blow over. Major Javet, the Adjutant here, has
been the soul of kindness. He believes that Poilu and I
were going to be married and he has been offering his
condolences ever since. All the same, I suspect he is
not displeased by the sudden removal of his chief.
Javet, nice young man that he is, has been interested in
me for a long time, and I feel we shall get on well
together.

I write you a letter now because I shall be gone by
the time you recover. If you are ever in this part of the
world again, I shall be happy to see you.

And now, a last word about the present letter. You
must surrender it as soon as you have read it to the
servant who delivers it. Until you have done so neither
you nor Miss Seferis will be allowed to leave. You
understand, there must be no compromising evidence
to interfere with the smooth running of ben Tahar's
trial. Please don't be difficult about this. It would

grieve me if anything were to happen to you following
your refusal to surrender this letter.

Sincerely yours,
Rirha bent Ali

I had no sooner finished reading the letter when
the Arab girl who had brought it returned with the
empty plate. Without hesitation I laid the letter back
on it. The girl smiled and left without a word. A few
moments later she returned with my passport, my
wallet and my various weapons, all of which had
been taken from me on the train journey to
Ghardaia.

I lit a cigarette after she had disappeared for the
third time. I had been lucky. It struck me suddenly
that I was definitely 'off form'. Had I played such a
foolish hand in any one of fifty situations in the past,
I should have been dead long ago. On the other
hand, the fact that the situation had come to such
quick resolution did not surprise me at all. Situations,
complex as they may be, are in the habit of being
resolved, just like that, simply because their complex-
ity makes for instability. In this instance, as in countless others, the resolution took place in a matter of
hours. I had achieved—though I can take little com-
mendation for it—what I set out to do, namely to
find Helen Seferis and to set her at liberty. Or was
that last part of my design? I smiled. From what I
had seen of Miss Seferis, I could not imagine ever
wishing to set her at liberty. I closed my eyes and
tried to picture her. It came to me only as I fell again
into sleep.

Chapter 10

Once again I was flying above the clouds that collected in cotton-tufts beyond the wing-tips. Tufts which, as they neared the underbelly of the aircraft, were dissipated in strands of vapor which lay for a moment against the windows and then broke to disclose an endless stretch of blue; but this time I was not travelling alone. On the seat next to me, near the window, was Helen Seferis whose long lashed eyes were visible above her superb cheekbones as she turned towards me again.

"You say you've read the whole manuscript?"

I smiled.

"Every word," I said. "Some of it, twice over."

"And you got the impression that I had succeeded?"

"In depersonalizing yourself?"

"Yes, in becoming a plant almost, a kind of melting of intellectual marrow, so that I existed only in my thighs and in my sex...you know what I mean."

"Well, did you?"

She smiled. "All right," she said, "if you won't commit yourself, I'll go on where the diary left off..."

"At a very dramatic point, if I remember rightly!"

"No, seriously, Anthony, don't laugh. It was a kind of self-prostration and it did work, while I remained at the brothel, that is. I tell you, I had ceased to be in the ordinary sense of the word. I lived through my five senses night after night, and the days too, for the effect of the drug never really wore off. I seldom bothered to get out of bed, never between men, and only for a few hours each day. An incredible lassitude came over me, centered about my loins—I could smell myself, I didn't find it unpleasant, not after the first few weeks anyway, and the men never complained. And when I was feeling most sexual, it was as though a hand lay on them, continually, its fingers at work in my hair which grew more thickly and my thighs were really yellow, yellow and plump against it, and then I would look down over my navel and I would see my own hand, set like a little octopus among the hairs, and I'd feel a sudden excitement, a kind of fizz, at the base of my spine and a kind of faint lingering itch in the downy skin of my thighs and belly just below the navel where the hairs start, and that would cause my fingers to move, tentatively at first, like a man who groped me in a cinema once, and then I would thrust in with three or four fingers, suddenly, and always so easily! Always. It's strange, Anthony, almost like a spiderweb as you open your fingers afterwards, only it gleamed and was sticky in a different way, more oily and less dry. And there I'd stop. I didn't want to spoil the night! And anyway, the lassitude came over me again. I almost forgot to be sexual—imagine! Forgot! One minute it was as though my sex would burst, like a pleasant kind of ulcer inside somewhere that threatens to burst into a pain at the slightest increase of intensity, and then next minute completely calm, running my fingers softly over my belly, fingers inside my cunt, and then holding them at my nose and lips and inhaling myself, tasting my juice. Smell, touch, taste and sight. Hearing only necessary at the point of the orgasm or an occasional sigh, soundless almost as a new level of pressure and pleasure was reached in the pit of my belly. Really, I did become my senses! I was just an existing shell with sense, probing my own existence through my cunt, my mouth, my asshole. The deep rich scent of sex that lived between my legs became my soul. My fingers, playing inside my own inner sanctum, became my savior."

"And the nights?"

Helen laughed. "You are interested, Mr. Harvest?"

I scrutinized her. Her superb, soft blonde hair tumbled in a silver cascade over the black, neatly costumed shoulders, and her full lovely lips were soft and wet as she smiled her insinuation. Her grey eyes were gentle and passionate at the same time. I leaned forward to kiss her. Her smartly gloved hand held me at a safe distance, the slender fingers as soft as petals at my mouth and chin, as her eyes surveyed mine, half inviting, half scornful of my move.

"The nights, Mr. Harvest, were very long, very hot, and my body perspired freely on the sheepskin mattress. The way you moved your head forward just now reminds me of one lover, practically the only one whom I could distinguish, who used to begin by laying his face between my thighs, low down, so that when he put his tongue out it was almost between my knees. He used to wear about a week's stubble. Oh, what he did was wonderful. He moved so slowly, breathing, tonguing. I was mad with desire by the time he forced my thighs apart to contain me in his mouth. And then upwards again over my belly, past my navel, and he would take one of my nipples in his mouth at the same time as I felt myself parted, not roughly, very gently, and then he was in.

"He would press the huge, dark head of his manhood up to the front of my opening and would linger there, gingerly, as if to collect the dew of my wet cunt and tease me. Yet he wasn't really teasing, he was teaching me, in a way, a kind of receptiveness, which, when I mastered it, was actually a great power. In many ways it is a great power over men. Yet you wouldn't tell by looking at me, at first, as I was a wriggling, trapped, sex-starved nymph at first, because I wanted that cock so bad, so deeply implanted in me. But then, I learned to let nature take his course.

"And this lover, once inside, would press himself to the very hilt in such a way that with each movement, each stroke, my cunt would feel quite close to coming, and I would be so fulfilled, so filled up. Even if he stopped midway, I would feel as if I had all that I needed.

"And that is when he would give the most. He'd pull me to him by the hips, and press my clit-bud against his groin by grasping me in such a way that it created a delicious pressure. He wouldn't fuck me, he'd rock inside me, tipping his cock back and forth, to and fro, rather than pulling it in and out.

"My lips would swell around the organ, and they'd swell up fast because the excitement was so great, and this would increase his pleasure so—to be drawn in so snugly by my cunt—that he would want to please me more. And it was quite lovely.

"Almost always, when he would feel my cunt coming ever-so-close to an explosion, he would very gently pull out and return his lips to my quivering inner pussy lips and kiss—just kiss, lightly, softly, upon the bud of my swollen clitoris, until I was quite wild with desire, my inner cunt walls throbbing and burning.

"My legs would shake, my knees tremble, and the inner thighs would quiver gently, and then shake uncontrollably, as he laid his sweet kisses onto my swollen little knob.

"And, somehow, he knew the precise, exact moment to take the little quivering button into the warmth of his mouth, between his lips, and begin to suck, meanwhile the stubble of his beard would rub against the lips of my sex and create an additional excitement.

"He would cup my ass cheeks in his big hands, and draw my bottom to his face, press my cunt to his mouth, and would suck on my clit with great attention to bring forth the most exquisite orgasms I've ever known. And then, just as he would draw the creamy emission from me, is when I would press myself quite forcefully into his face. And with a sensual, sweeping motion, he would relax the tight puckering of his mouth, and, opening his jaw, would take my whole cunt in, devouring me, eating all of me. His hands, firmly on my bottom, pressed up, and his mouth, firmly pressed like a suction cup on my entire sex, created the most delicious sandwich. And it gave him great joy to then lick from my cunt the juice of my spending, lapping up his accomplishments in a sense.

He had the most extraordinary way, in fact, of inserting his tongue after I came, that would, in a mere flash, bring me right back to the pitch of desire and excitement that I experienced right before my orgasm. Ah, that tongue...

"Oh, the nights were endless, and the day was the same. I was right out of time."

"And what happened then?"

"What do you mean. After his tongue was in?"

"No," I exclaimed with a laugh. "I didn't mean that at all! I meant how did you get out of the brothel. What happened from your point of view?"

"Well, one night a man arrived. At first we made love, just as I did with all the rest, and then, afterwards, he asked me if I remembered him. I didn't. There were so many, and as I say, personality had ceased to interest me, either my own or my lovers'. I didn't know him at all. Then he said it was he who had taken my diary and I remembered. I laughed. I had long since ceased to lay any importance to its loss. But then he said he was an agent of the Chief of Police at Ghardaia and that he was here officially to take me out of the brothel and return me to civilization. At first I didn't understand. I had almost forgotten what it was like before I came to the brothel. Time had been continuous and indivisible…it was all day and endless, and it was only when I made a great effort that I could remember anything. My bed was my world and the people in it were the women who fed me and my lovers. I was a little afraid of ben Tahar."

"Yes, and what then?"

"Well, he meant what he said. It was Colonel Poilu who had sent him. So I had to go. The big Arab woman who fed me was very upset and kept kissing me and wishing me good luck, but it was obvious that ben Tahar had already arranged with whomever owned the brothel that I should leave."

"And then you came to Ghardaia?"

"Yes. We were two or three days on the road, perhaps more. I don't remember exactly. Everything was very strange after life in the brothel. Suddenly to be out in the open air again, all day long, and in a tent at night instead of my little room in the brothel. That was endless. My window was a mere slit. I would stand there at sunset and watch the red glow on the white roofs and listen for the noises of people in the streets below. But I don't remember ever wanting to be with them. After that, the tent was strange."

"With ben Tahar?"

"Of course. He was a good lover. He made me dance for him naked. There were three of them actually. One of them played a kind of bagpipe and the other a fiddle. Ben Tahar himself just smoked and watched. I had learned belly dancing from the girl with whom I was closeted before I arrived at the brothel. I danced as well as I could and then they held me down and each had his turn with me. I enjoyed it thoroughly. Does that surprise you? How deeply they sank into me! It was superb the way they did it. Two of them would hold me in position, each with the palm of one hand under one buttock, lifting my lower torso about a foot off the ground, and with their other hands gripping me behind my thighs just above the knees, pulling me open and upwards for the one who was fucking me. God, the sensations I felt. They had a way of increasing the size of their members. They would oil my belly, and sometimes they sprinkled some fine white sand over my belly and loins and that acted as an irritant. Every time I rose to meet the thrust of the man who was taking me I would feel the hands of the other two clench at the soft parts of my buttocks and pull downward at the backs of my thighs so that the spine of the third penetrated even more deeply, and they would be chanting, a kind of series of inarticulate grunts, to keep time with the rhythm of our loins. After all three had taken me, I would be exhausted and they would make me smoke hashish and try to rouse me again.

"Then one night, they led in a large, black-skinned man. They explained that he was a visiting Caliph from a distant land who spoke no local or European language. The men were not unpleasant. If I pleased the Caliph, they said, they would give me all kinds of presents. Honey and almonds, strange crystalized fruits, a kind of sherbet, and even some nicely wrought Arab jewelry. But when the Caliph removed his clothes, I was afraid. But there was no possibility of escape. One of the men held me firmly by the wrist and pointed to the Caliph's member. It was huge. A kind of blueish-greyish-black color, as thick as my forearm with a huge mushroom-like nob on the end. I had heard of such huge members, but I had never dreamed of having one inside me. The Caliph bade me to caress it, and they all laughed when they saw my hesitation. The Caliph barked something in his foreign tongue and stamped his feet like a bull. His huge phallus rose up and down as though it was attached to his underbelly by a system of delicate springs. Then one of the men took me—I was naked—and held me roughly across his knees, rubbing a ball of mutton fat at my sex for a few minutes, to ease the Caliph's entry. The Caliph came over and examined it. He grinned and nodded at me. I tried to smile back, but I was afraid of this man. He was big, with pitch black skin, and he smelled of a combination of sweat, poor personal hygiene and musk. But I had no time for thought and knew it would be useless to protest. I was laid down for the pleasure of the big black man, my bottom raised by one man on each side until my mutton-greased sex was wide open and ready. The Caliph climbed atop me, hoisting himself over me with huge, strong arms. He positioned himself over my cunt until it was up close to his huge cock.

"The Caliph panted with lust. The men behind me pushed me upward, spread me open more. I felt the huge nob slip from between my thighs and ride over my belly, and then come closer to my cunthole. The men grabbed hold of the Caliph's cock with one hand and heaving up my buttocks with the other, brought our sexes together again. A moment later, I felt the huge, black mushroom head press past my opening, and begin to dive deep into my cunt. The cock felt as if it would split my pelvis. The men were all grinning. The Caliph snorted some foreign sounding grunt and stood rigid for a moment, then began to buck wildly. I felt my cunt being crushed beneath his thrusts and closed my eyes and tried to feel pleasure. Ben Tahar noticed my effort and told me to grab the Caliph's back. I did so, raising my own naked belly flat against the Caliph's. This appeared to excite him even more. He bucked wildly. At the same time I felt my ankles gripped like the handles of a wheelbarrow by the man who stood behind the Caliph's rump and I was pulled deeply upon his member, my cunt clinging over his cock like a stocking to a leg. My thighs and belly were lathered with sweat. I heard the Caliph moan, felt him press himself into me fully and suddenly my thighs and sex were inundated with his passion. Amidst his moans and jolts, my cunt was pressed tight against his groin, as if to collect every ounce of jism. Then I could feel that my cunt was stretched to the limit by his huge dong. The Caliph was shuddering. A crystal dripped from his diminished phallus. Without a word, he put his clothes back on and left the tent. Then the men laughed. Ben Tahar gave me a hashish cigarette and I was left to rest in peace for the remainder of the night. I don't remember anything else beyond that.

"The following day ben Tahar handed me over to Colonel Poilu."

"Did he act like all the others?"

"No, on the contrary, I didn't appear to interest him. I asked him when I could make arrangement to journey to Paris, telling him that if he contacted Nadya Pamandari there or her father in Bombay, the necessary funds would be sent. When I had finished he was laughing."

"Why?"

"Because of course he had no intention of giving me my liberty. Zarouk wanted me for his harem."

"Zarouk had a harem?"

"It wasn't large, about six women apart from myself. I was the only white woman. The rest were Arab women except for one Egyptian girl. A harem is an amazing place. It smells of women, like a large dressing room filled with chorus girls, filled with sweat and perfume, obstinately female, naked flesh, soiled cloth and then there is the laughter. They are mostly fat, plump and white from the special diet of oil and semolina; the skins have an unhealthy colour and the odor is a peculiar one, pungent, repellent and exciting at the same time. The women quarrel and make love amongst themselves. We had a enunuch, a boy of about sixteen, very fat, with slow, sly eyes, and in spite of the fact that he wasn't a man, all the women were in love with him. It was he who conducted the chosen wife to Zarouk's quarters, and then he would return and play with the women who remained. They fought like cats and dogs over him. I always thought that a eunuch was sexless. Ali wasn't. He was much more lecherous than he would have been if he hadn't been castrated. He caressed the women for hours, with his tongue and with his fingers, taking great delight in raising them almost to the pitch of their excitement and then abandoning them for another. I saw two or three of them crawling naked about the floor, like large whitish slugs trying to hold Ali by the ankle. He would kick them away and choose another. Sometimes he would only make love to them if they allowed him to whip them first. He did not use a cane. He used a long thong of hide, black and thick. I had never seen women reduced to such a state of subservience."

"Did he whip you?"

Helen laughed.

"Never," she said, "because I had no need of him. Zarouk usually called for me. The others were very jealous of me and one day they asked Ali to whip me. All six of them threw themselves on me and tore off my clothes. They held my face down on the floor, their big thighs bent at the knees and not a few of them showing the barb between their thighs as they squatted over me, and they called on Ali to come with his whip and teach me a lesson. He was delighted by the idea. Out of the corner of my eye I saw him take the whip and advance towards me. Fortunately, he spoke French and I told him that if he struck me it would leave a mark and that I would show it to Zarouk and he would flog him.

He hesitated and then he set about the six women who were holding me down, lashing out right and left for all he was worth and sending them squealing into corners. One night when Zarouk was away, the little Egyptian girl came over to where I was lying and began to caress my back. The poor child had not been out of the harem for some months. Zarouk appeared to have no interest in her, which was surprising because she was much prettier than the rest. Ali too didn't appear to have any interest in her. She lay beside me, pressing her softness against me and imploring me not to send her away. She was skillful in her love-making. When finally I looked at her, she had already bared her breasts. She was fragile and animal at the same time. Her breasts were smooth and of a light sepia colour, not unlike Nadya's, with the same dark, rubbery nipples, the same taut poise which gave to the lean line of her belly which ran away beneath them an even more sinuous and pregnant appearance. I caressed them first with my hands and then with lips, feeling the delicately scented rubberish tissue with the pad of my tongue before cupping the breasts upwards in my hands, I sucked them until they stood stiff and rampant, two phallic nobbles against which my hair fell like a silver veil. The poor girl was delirious. The soft, fragrant odor of her belly and thighs rose up to me as she peeled off the rest of her clothes for my caressing lips. With my tongue, I traced the soft line of fur which ran from the little scented pit of her delicately whorled navel to the smooth delta of blue-black hair which lay like a ferny plateau between the chubbed hotness of her thighs. Her torso was bristling with passion as I raised it to my lips. She was groaning and the fats of her thighs were quivering to every slight pressure of my tongue. How lovely it was to smell her young, craving lust which mingled with the exotic scents and ointments she used in her toilette. I almost developed a passion for her. She wanted so frantically to be loved by me, struggling almost like a woman in labor to widen herself to my caress. It is impossible to describe. It was as though she felt herself imprisoned and were fighting to pries herself free. With one hand I worked gently at the mastic substance which rose through her prickling hairs until the whole sheath of her lower body throbbed beneath a lather of sweat and passion. As she gripped me even more strongly, I abandoned myself to her and my own thighs became hot and flaccid as the desire to be with her in her ecstasy manifested itself in a radiant, almost painful gyration at my sex. Our wet skins mingled. The hair under our armpits became damp as our sinuous limbs wrestled like trees' creepers to be close, and then, suddenly almost, she uttered a little cry in her throat and softened beneath me, her haunches unclenching themselves, as her desire slipped upwards to another less urgent dimension. I shall never forget her final shudders, the exquisite corrosions which passed through her body as she strove to be co-existent with me. I caressed her for a long time afterwards. She was as grateful as a child."

At that moment, Helen laughed. "What am I telling you all this for!" she said. "You haven't told me anything at all about yourself!" She looked out of the window at the pure stretch of blue sky on which there was no longer any suspicion of cloud.

"What is there to say?" I began. "Nadya employed me to find you and bring you back to civilization. Through no fault of my own, I seem to have managed it."

"How did you meet Nadya?"

I explained at length how I had been engaged to look after her by Lord Grisskillin. She asked me if I had met Mario Ratsonli. I told her what had happened at the party and she said: "Poor Mario! I'm sure he needed the money. I wonder what he's doing now?"

"And Nadya," I echoed.

"Little Nadya," Helen said, "are you in love with her, Anthony?"

"If I were, I certainly shouldn't let you know about it. From what I heard, you disposed of the last suitor in a rather drastic way."

"He disposed of himself, or rather, dispatched himself. I don't consider myself in any way to blame."

Helen was magnificent. I have never seen a woman so completely desirable. Her blonde hair was smooth, like mercury at the sides of her superbly classical face, the cheekbones high, the eyes larger and more almond-shaped than one would have thought possible. She was dressed immaculately in a fine black linen costume, her magnificent thighs crossed and her slender ankles rising out of four inch high-heeled shoes.

It occurred to me, like a sudden shock that I had never made love to her. I had listened to the almost archaic expression of her lust as she described in detail the fantastic episode in which she had been involved, and I had read every page of her manuscript in which she had described every crevice of her lovely body. But that was all. Words. Not direct experience.

She read my thoughts.

"I have the unwarrantable feeling that you and I are very much alike, Anthony!"

"In what way?" I said with a grin.

"Flesh. Lust. Sexual exertion. Love, perhaps," Helen said slowly.

"I'd like to think so," I said wryly.

"What? You have asked me to marry you and you don't know?"

"Did I?"

"Didn't you?"

"Would you like me to ask you again?"

"What was my reply the first time?"

"You said we must wait until we got to know one another better."

She laughed.

"The pleasure of the masquerade is done when we come to show our faces!" she said.

Epilogue
by Helen Seferis

I have told all about my life in my diary. Its color has remained as always. I speak now only of what I told Anthony on the night on which we arrived in Tangiers.

We had been dancing. Not yet lovers after nearly a week of acquaintance—Anthony took a few days to recover from his 'execution'—we glided about the floor, our thighs touching; and for me, anyway, a sudden knowledge of freedom in the arms of a man I felt sure I could love was the greatest pleasure I had known for many months, a pleasure which, quite distinct from the close sensual secrecy as my buttocks had raised themselves from the sheepskin, filled my whole being because it was born of the sense of possibility. A whole acre of love lay before me! It was not the pleasure of a moment, like the feel of another's sex: It was the sense of the infinite possibility of those moments. Anthony was smiling. I knew he loved me even then. I told him I felt very young suddenly. "But of course you are!" he said. Was I? I didn't know. I didn't know how long I had been in North Africa! I laughed to cover my embarrassment. I hadn't felt young. Nadya was young but I was not. But with the new sense of freedom everything had changed. I didn't feel young. I was young!

"Take me home," I said.

We walked through the crowd of dancers and Anthony went to fetch my wrap. I lit a cigarette. Rather I was just about to light it when a small fat hand with a gold snake ring which I recognized thrust itself under my face with a cigarette lighter. I gasped and looked up. Zarouk was smiling pleasantly.

"My dear Helen!" he said with genuine delight, "What good fortune to see you here! You are alone?"

"I'm afraid not."

"Ah, what a pity! You wouldn't care to walk out on him?"

I shook my head.

"Who is he? Some fool no doubt?"

"Anthony Harvest," I replied. "I believe you met him once."

"To think that I could have killed him once!" said Zarouk affably. It was difficult not to admire his poise. This bloated man who had forced my body into all manner of positions and given it some of its sharpest of sexual sensations, who had maltreated me and doted on me for a number of months, who was wanted by the police throughout nearly all of North Africa, had the audacity to be standing in the brightly lit foyer of a well known nightclub in Tangiers.

"I can't believe you love me as you used to my

dear," he went on, "if you would forsake me for a young fool like that!"

At that moment Anthony appeared with my wrap. He too was smiling.

"Hullo, Zarouk! Have they not hanged you yet?"

"I have yet to experience that pleasure, replied Zarouk politely. "I fear I might take a long time to die."

"I'm not an expert on the subject," Anthony said, "but I have no doubt it will be a long time before they are clever enough to put your head into a noose."

"Haha...haha..." said Zarouk, "I take it back, Helen! This young man is not a fool. He might be quite bright. I wonder whether he would be bright enough to be interested in a proposition?"

"Not tonight, Zarouk."

"There," said Zarouk to Anthony. "Helen has spoken for you. Goodnight, my dear! Goodnight, Harvest."

We watched him waddle through the foyer and into an inner room. Anthony took my arm and we walked outside and called a cab.

When we were seated Anthony said: "What kind of man is he, Helen?"

It would be difficult to describe him. Sometimes he looked ridiculous. But only through civilized eyes, the eyes of Western civilization even. For in North Africa he was by no means ridiculous. Clever, often powerful, evidently rich, and more important to a woman, the most imaginative of lovers. I can feel his hand now, the first time he touched me. His right hand, like a claw, took me just above my knee. The balls of his fingers pressed into the muscle, firmly but not harshly, and then his other hand was beneath my skirt and hard, like a piece of rock, between my thighs.

"Lie still, Helen," he said.

I allowed my body to relax, closing my eyes and allowing fear to be converted by desire into lust. I breathed slowly and deeply. His hands caressed my body above my clothes for a long time before he began to undress me. Then his nimble fingers were unfastening my clothes and drawing them off, garment by garment, until my naked body lay before him like a sorcerer's experiment. I had never before known such a delicate touch. He was sitting at my feet with one of my legs raised on his lap and the pressure of his fingers on the slow muscles of my thighs caused desire to overtake the whole compact thickness of my lower torso like a paralysis. He played me like an instrument, impinging at my more delicate surfaces, his actions making themselves known only by the electricity of his touch. His face was obsessed, like that of a religious maniac. I closed my eyes again and came to exist as a cone of experience, tremulous at the point at which his sense of me entered, a supple finger in a soft, wet hole, and my whole lower belly became ignited, my cunt a dull ache at my center and carried upwards towards his lust by the eager reflex action of my soft muscles. My buttocks left the divan and his small hand was underneath them, sharp as a shatter of glass, holding, exerting pressures, and controlling the tenseness of my wheat-colored abdomen. Then his lips were there, teasing the sap through every aching fibre and causing my body to arch insanely towards its master. Again and again I felt the knot of intensity at the pit of me gather and exfoliate from every soft leaf and vine, stirring the dregs of my lust about the smooth beaker of my belly, causing a thin and delirious sap of pleasure to mount into twin poles of excruciating pleasure at my nipples which his mouth took and tongued to rigidity. I was suddenly aware that he had brought everything to the surface, every shy recess with its nerve-struts, like a summer parasol reversed by wind, and at each of his fingers a rumor which drove darkly into my blood and was carried like an urgent heat in streams which reached my extremities. When his lips touched and broke into me, I emitted a gasp of pleasure. At the same time, a marish lassitude inhabited my flanks as though the little atoll at which his lips worked were a sun, and I given over to it on a warm summer beach. His tongue moved on my bud of desire with a fierce intensity, licking, stroking, talking possession of my sex and sucking me into his mouth as if to claim ownership. At that point, I felt my other center pierced, suddenly, almost roughly, and the pain ran like a fire through my drugged flesh, until it was no longer pain, but cool, a lymphatic irrigation, as he pressed a finger into my asshole, taking license to enter, to expand, to shove me full of his flesh. I felt my tears dry on my cheeks. Then, still without speaking, he was himself naked, and I felt the soft bowl of his belly like a caress on my own and his short arms raised me from behind until, my legs spread-eagled like a distended pair of compasses, his hard huge nob gouged itself against my sex. There was a constriction at my belly and I breathed heavily. My breasts quivered beneath his weight as he bore downward on me with the power of fat and muscle until I was pinioned like a butterfly beneath his heavy and subtle gestures of fertility. My speech was inarticulate. I fought and gave way. In response to the strange and extravagant intrusion, my sweating body attained a luxuriance which I had not dreamt was possible. Cords slackened, tensions relaxed; my seam broke outward to give of its fertile depths. And I spread my cunt wide open to his

219

approach, accepting hungrily, the weapon of his desires. He pressed in, deeply, burying the shaft deep within the walls of my love chamber. I rode against his cock, pressed against his flesh, greeted every thrust with hoisted, hungry hips. And then my hands were caressing his head and our lips mingled in a caress which soothed the lavish gyration which went relentlessly on at the crux of my sex. His tongue slipped into the depths of my mouth, rounding my teeth, sucking my tongue, and we kissed, our mouths plastered to one another, tongues entwined, for what seemed an eternity.

The confederacy of our motion was infinite. Again and again my seed was responsive to his motions, to the hot flux and reflux on the strange female graphite which he had divined and now drew from my flesh. His short hairs prickled at my belly, and inner lips, stimulating me to new efforts in my lust to bring his phallic spine even closer at my furrow and his last hard movement, interpreted by my body as the symptom of imminent emission from his, caused every valve of my carnality to be flooded with the sap of erotic sensation; my thighs, like toppling pilings crashed upwards and aside as a vast surge of pleasure seized me in a melting hold of delirium. My come poured out in juicy, creamy spurts, as did his. We lay in the mingled wetness of our spent desires.

That was my first experience of him. But he did not stop there. He rose from my shuddering body and, crossing the room, returned with a kind of metal-studded harness.

"Don't be afraid, my dear," he said softly as he put it on. "You will find it strange at first, but the ecstasy that follows is like something you have never experienced." The harness came in four bands round the fleshy parts of my body and as I watched it being strapped on I suddenly caught sight of a rubber lead which ran to a transformer and an electric contact at the base of one of the walls. I screamed out in alarm. But it was too late. Once again his soft body nuzzled me open as his sex sought mine and his strong fat arms prohibited my escape. I clutched him close, knowing that whatever current passed through me would pass through him also. He smiled in pleasure as he felt the strength of my embrace. "Don't be afraid," he said again. "Give yourself over to it."

The first shock made me almost retch with pain, and yet seduced me with a somewhat curious pleasure. My flanks rose madly upwards and sank again below his crushing weight. I was sweating freely and all the surface flesh of our bodies was shuddering uncontrollably. He was lisping something which sounded like an incantation in my ear. I allowed myself to relax and enjoy the after-effects of the sudden terrible tension. A few moments later, when we had calmed down, our flesh tremulous and quietly sensating, he again worked the contact. This time, the dull ache spread like a splintering disease throughout my body, almost causing my heart to stop beating, and then the ringing, sweating after-effect supervened and our flesh met and quivered in a jelloid haze of receptivity. Our passion was growing again. The soft gimbals of my buttocks moved tentatively upwards and coaxed a reaction. Softly and wetly we experienced, the hairs of our bodies now stiff as grass and wet with the perspiration of our pain. The third and last time that he operated the switch was perhaps the most intense of all. The switch was constructed with a spring so that when the pressure of the hand was relaxed contact was broken. As the third invasion electrified our bodies, I saw his cheek muscles bulge in his frantic effort to permit a huge charge of electricity to live in us before the switch fell from his nerveless grasp to the floor. For a moment we lay motionless and paralyzed. Then, as the sweat seeped from between our pressed skin, and we were again in control of our limbs' movements, desire returned and we made love quietly and with a sense of softened finality which was excruciating. The relaxation of our bodies after the seizing invasion was a much more ultimate thing, and the soft corrosion of our lust as our bellies rose and fell together with the slackness of relief was a much more reassuring thing than passion, for me at least, had ever been before. Zarouk's body was a pure instrument of love, in spite of its obesity, in spite of the stupid aesthetic judgment that an essentially puritan civilization would have passed upon it. For that night, I lay in his arms like a child spilling over with pure sensual delight, the calmness, the weakness of our bodies after the electrical attack causing us to blend in a kind of cosmic sympathy of pure sensuality, and, as his seed entered my loins, I drew him as close as my straining arms were able to, and my soft wet thighs, bearing my warm sex, rose upwards in complete adoration. I remember he stroked me for a long time afterwards, and I remember thinking how adult was his sense of love.

Anthony, to whom I told all this and much more, first in the taxi and then more secretly as our bodies met for the first time in the mauve silence of the hotel room—I remember there was a neon sign which cast a helio light across the street and spilled a purplish shadow across our floor—was able at once to comprehend the kind of giving of which I spoke, and his own hands, flitting softly about my breasts and loins, coaxed me again to experience my deepest delirium. But from Anthony, that first night at least, I did not desire the sensational. I did not desire to be transported on a garish lust, the better to bring about a final union. The union, born of a week's abstinence, was more than perfect, and his superb virility coupled close to my dark female desire, was in itself a more lovely thing than a hundred abortive attempts to achieve strange levels of excitement. It was for me the end of a long journey and the beginning of a new voyage of delight, across tender sensual seas which were hitherto unexplored, and into subterranean depths which were richer in ore for the fact that I wanted to be for this man what he wanted me to be.

We bathed together in a large, pink-tile tub and in the soapy waters I playfully took hold of his cock. I moved so that I was kneeling above him in the tub, and, facing him, took the handsome face of my hero, my savior, and deeply kissed the lips, pressing mine on top of them without yet opening my mouth.

Softly, I bent down to the hairy, manly chest and kissed the somewhat wet, curly hair and placed my mouth upon the nipples. Gently, I sucked on them as I ran my fingers through the hairs.

I wanted more kisses from the brave and shrewd investigator who had assured my liberty. I went to his mouth and now, opening my own, pressed my tongue against his until the two were like instruments of passion, entwined in a hot, wet, sensual attack. I pulled his head toward me from behind, softly, and pressed my tongue further into his. We lapped at one another for almost a half hour, cemented in our passions by our sweet kisses.

The heat in my belly rose from the feeling of wanting so to share, to experience, to be one with Anthony. And he, too, wanted the same with me.

I positioned myself above his hard, rampant tool as he sat propped comfortably in the tub and proceeded to insert him into my love box, and grip it to me with a squeeze of my muscles. I was wet between the legs, juicy, and it was so thick and lubricated that even the soapy water did not dry me up. I pressed down on my lover's cock and within moments, he was all inside me, buried far into the burrows of my love snatch. He groaned his pleasure, feeling his cock drawn inward and sheathed as if it were a hot dog pressed inside the perfect sized bun.

We didn't move much; we gently rocked. My arms were wrapped around his neck, and he was bent over, kissing my breasts, taking the titties in his hands and sucking the nipple buds between his lips, and licking them, softly, slowly, engagingly.

The juicy opening of my canal continued to seep with love juice, and Anthony and I kept rocking gently in one another's arms, cock to cunt, pressed tightly in unison.

He lifted his face to mine and again our tongues met as our mouths, fully opened, pressed and pressed tongue against tongue, as if fighting to be rammed down a throat. I sucked his tongue as if it were his cock. My cunt muscles, involuntarily, began to squeeze around his organ in excitement. I felt him squeeze back, as if his cock were a baseball bat, taking a swing in the first base of my lower bush.

My cunt was quite on fire; his cock was as well, I could tell by the huge, hard, swell of it. And as much as we were compelled to push, and gyrate against one another, we both instead surrendered to the softness of the moment, the notion that all we had to do was 'be.'

I spread my legs just a little wider, squatting just a little further apart and planted myself on his huge, engorged organ just a little deeper. I could feel him touching the very endings of my nerves, the very soul of my sexuality, and I allowed the pressing feeling of his prick to pierce my inner sanctum without moving to ease the intensity.

Simultaneously, my clit bud, now an enlarged, swollen knob, was pressing up against the short hairs of his groin, rubbing up against the fierceness of his desire.

It made my cunt quiver, and, as my body again reacted with an involuntary squeeze, I could feel his cock slide in just a bit further, pressing as it was pulled in by the enticements of my sex.

Our nipples rubbed against one another now, the tiny buds of his, the soft pink buds of mine, finding each other amidst the mesh of his hairy chest, my fleshy titties, and the bath water that got between us. Pressed together so exquisitely, with our organs totally devoted to the oneness they were experiencing, we were quickly being swept away into the blissful thunder of desire; it was inching up our thighs, our inner legs, our groins, our asses, our organs.

In a heated moment, the kissing, which had started tenderly, picked up a faster, more urgent pace. And Anthony began pressing his cock with a bit more energy, more forcefulness; I got the sense that he could not stop, did not want to stop.

On my knees in the tub, positioned over him as I was, next trying to pry myself as far apart as possible, pushing my legs against the sides of the tub as if it would stretch, to insure that the whole of Anthony's manhood, the all of him, every inch of him, was stuffed as deeply inside me as physically possible.

There was no franticness, no wildly gyrating motion, just an urgency to be totally filled by him, and to give to him the pleasure of being totally received and taken in by my cunt.

We looked one another in the eyes for a very long time, and, without speaking, began to quietly allow the dams of sexual pressure that had been building in our groins to be released, simultaneously, and thus, we intuitively began to slowly, sensually, softly move together in such a way that the deep passions of our sexual souls could begin their fiery eruptions throughout our lower parts.

I held on, still, to the back of his neck. He gripped me at the hips and ever so gently pressed me downward, even more, and began to slowly rock my hips back and forth so that my cunt rubbed up against his groin as his cock filled me fully. I could feel it pressed against my inner organs, feel it joyously jabbing at them, touching them. And next, the swollen bud of my clitoris was rubbing deliciously against his groin as he rocked me, and I could feel ecstasy start in the very tip, the very end of my clit and then could feel it begin to work its way upward, into my entire lower belly.

But I didn't have to move, for Anthony moved my hips back and forth, slightly, and pressed himself in me in such a way that I was totally filled, totally fulfilled, and totally taken.

I looked into his eyes and he into mine. I could feel my face contracting slightly into a twist of abandoned pleasure, and his did too, as our breathing increased and our chests heaved, pressing our titties and nipples together still.

Inevitably our dual pleasure, our dance of oneness, culminated this first time in a grand, yet softly explosive finale. And we kept holding one another's glance, and holding one another, as our cunt and cock began the blissful spasms of orgasm through the sheer, intense, connection and closeness—as opposed to any pounding, or fucking or heaving and thrusting.

I was gripped very quickly once the orgasm really took hold, and Anthony seemed to be as well. For the soft panting came from us both, the light pressing from us both, and the gentle squeezing, again, from us both, as we exploded onto a magic carpet of delightful contact between the souls of our sexes. The emissions from us both trickled white drops of juice into the bath water.

We were shriveled all over from being in the water so long, and were awed by the intensity of our first experience in lovemaking. For all the wild fucks we'd both had in our adventures, none could come close to the true sharing of our sex, as it had in this abundant moment in time.

Next morning, when we stepped into the plane for Paris, I was quite certain that neither Nadya nor any other woman could hope to take him from me. I had never been in Paris before. A new city and a new lover—I required nothing else to make the future spread out before me, glittering with the myriad colors of infinite possibility...

People are talking about:

The Masquerade Erotic Book Society Newsletter

◆ ◆ ◆ ◆ ◆ ◆ ◆ ◆ ◆ ◆ ◆ ◆ ◆ ◆ ◆ ◆ ◆ ◆ ◆ ◆

FICTION, ESSAYS, REVIEWS, PHOTOGRAPHY, INTERVIEWS, EXPOSÉS, AND MUCH MORE!

◆ ◆ ◆ ◆ ◆ ◆ ◆ ◆ ◆ ◆ ◆ ◆ ◆ ◆ ◆ ◆ ◆ ◆ ◆ ◆

"I received the new issue of the newsletter; it looks better and better."
—*Michael Perkins*

"I must say that yours is a nice little magazine, literate and intelligent."
—*HH, Great Britain*

"Fun articles on writing porn and about the peep shows, great for those of us who will probably never step onto a strip stage or behind the glass of a booth, but love to hear about it, wicked little voyeurs that we all are, hm? Yes indeed...."
—*MT, California*

"Many thanks for your newsletter with essays on various forms of eroticism. Especially enjoyed your new Masquerade collections of books dealing with gay sex."
—*GF, Maine*

"... a professional, insider's look at the world of erotica ..."
—*SCREW*

"I recently received a copy of *The Masquerade Erotic Book Society Newsletter*. I found it to be quite informative and interesting. The intelligent writing and choice of subject matter are refreshing and stimulating. You are to be congratulated for a publication that looks at different forms of eroticism without leering or smirking."
—*DP, Connecticut*

"Thanks for sending the books and the two latest issues of *The Masquerade Erotic Book Society Newsletter*. Provocative reading, I must say."
—*RH, Washington*

"Thanks for the latest copy of *The Masquerade Erotic Book Society Newsletter*. It is a real stunner."
—*CJS, New York*

THE MASQUERADE

EROTIC LIBRARY

DREAM CRUISE   *Gwenyth James*
Angelia has it all—a brilliant career and a beautiful face to match. But she
longs to kick up her high heels and have some fun, so she takes an island
vacation and vows to leave her sexual inhibitions behind. From the moment
her plane takes off, she finds herself in one hot and steamy encounter after
another, and her horny holiday doesn't end on Monday morning!   **30450**

RHINOCEROS BOOKS $6.95

THE MARKETPLACE   *Sara Adamson*
"Merchandise does not come easily to the Marketplace.... They haunt the
clubs and the organizations, their need so real and desperate that they
exude sensual tension when they glide through the crowds. Some of them
are so ripe that they intimidate the poseurs, the weekend sadists and the
furtive dilettantes who are so endemic to that world. And they never stop
asking where we may be found...."   **3096-2**

VENUS IN FURS   *Leopold von Sacher-Masoch*
This classic 19th century novel is the first uncompromising exploration of
the dominant/ submissive relationship in literature. The alliance of Severin
and Wanda epitomizes Sacher-Masoch's dark obsession with a cruel, controlling goddess and the urges that drive the man held in her thrall. Also
included in this volume are the letters exchanged between Sacher-Masoch
and Emilie Mataja—an aspiring writer he sought as the avatar of his forbidden desires.   **3089-X**

SENSATIONS   *Tuppy Owens*
A piece of porn history. Tuppy Owens tells the unexpurgated story of the
making of *Sensations*—the first big-budget sex flick. Originally commis-
sioned to appear in book form after the release of the film in 1975,
Sensations is finally released under Masquerade's stylish Rhinoceros
imprint. A document from a more reckless, bygone time!   **3081-4**

EVIL COMPANIONS   *Michael Perkins*
A handsome edition of this cult classic that includes a new preface by
Samuel R. Delany. Set in New York City during the tumultuous waning
years of the 60s, *Evil Companions* has been hailed as "a frightening classic."
A young couple explore the nether reaches of the erotic unconscious in a
shocking confrontation with the extremes of passion   **3067-9**

THE SECRET RECORD:Modern Erotic Literature   *Michael Perkins*
Michael Perkins, a renowned author and critic of sexually explicit fiction,
surveys the field with authority and unique insight. Updated and revised to
include the latest trends, tastes, and developments in this much-misunder-
stood genre.   **3039-3**

TOURNIQUET   *Alice Joanou*
"Remember," she said, "you were my father's pet, and now you are reduced
again as my slave until I feel you are worthy to service my pleasure. For
now you are my valet, my whipping post, and, if the whim takes me, an
object that fills my needs. Now kiss me and beg for forgiveness." At which
the slave kissed her extended hand and dropped to his knees.   **3067-9**

CANNIBAL FLOWER   *Alice Joanou*

"She is waiting in her darkened bedroom, as she has waited throughout history, to seduce and ultimately destroy the men who are foolish enough to be blinded by her irresistible charms. She is Salome, Lucrezia Borgia, Delilah—endlessly alluring, the fulfillment of your every desire. She will ensnare, entrap, and drive her willing victims to the cutting edge of ecstasy—and then devour them. She is the goddess of sexuality, and *Cannibal Flower* is her haunting siren song."—Michael Perkins   **72-6**

ILLUSIONS   *Daniel Vian*

Two disturbing tales of danger and desire on the eve of World War II. From private homes to lurid cafés to decaying streets, passion is explored, exposed, and placed in stark contrast to the brutal violence of the time. *Illusions* peels the frightened mask from the face of desire, and studies its changing features under the dim lights of a lonely Berlin evening. Unforgettable.   **3074-1**

MY DARLING DOMINATRIX   *Grant Antrews*

When a man and a woman fall in love it's supposed to be simple, uncomplicated, easy—unless that woman happens to be a dominatrix. This unpretentious love story captures the richness and depth of this very special kind of love. Devoid of sleaze or shame, this is an honest and heartbreaking story of the power and passion that binds human beings together. A must for every serious erotic library.   **3055-5**

LOVE IN WARTIME   *Liesel Kulig*

Madeleine knew that the handsome SS officer was a dangerous man. But she was just a cabaret singer in Nazi-occupied Paris, trying to survive in a perilous time. When Josef fell in love with her, he discovered that a beautiful, intelligent, and amoral woman can sometimes be even more dangerous than the fiercest warrior. A scalding, haunting, and utterly uncompromising look at forbidden passion.   **3044-X**

MASQUERADE BOOKS $4.95 EACH

GLORIA'S INDISCRETION   *Don Winslow*

"He looked up at her. Gloria stood passively, her hands loosely at her sides, her eyes still closed, a dreamy expression on her face ... She sensed his hungry eyes on her, could almost feel his burning gaze on her body, and she was aware of the answering lusty need in her loins...."   **3094-6**

HELLFIRE   *Charles G. Wood*

A vicious murderer is running amok in New York's sexual underground—and Nick O'Shay, a virile detective with the NYPD, plunges deep into the case. He soon becomes embroiled in an elusive world of fleshly extremes, hunting a madman seeking to purge America with fire and blood sacrifices. But the rules are different here, as O'Shay soon discovers.   **3085-7**

ROSEMARY LANE   *J.D. Hall*

The ups, downs, ins and outs of Rosemary Lane, an 18th century maiden named after the street in which she was abandoned as a child. Raised as the ward of Lord and Lady D'Arcy, after coming of age she discovers that her guardians' generosity is truly boundless—as they contribute heartily to her carnal education.   **3078-4**

HELOISE   *Sarah Jackson*

A panoply of sensual tales harkening back to the golden age of Victorian erotica. Desire is examined in all its intricacy, as fantasies are explored and urges explode. Innocence meets experience time and again in these passionate stories dedicated to the pleasures of the body. Sweetly torrid tales of erotic awakening!   **3073-3**

MASTER OF TIMBERLAND   *Sara H. French*
"Welcome to Timberland Resort," he began. "We are delighted that you have come to serve us. And you may all be assured that we will require service of you in the strictest sense. Our discipline is the most demanding in the world. You will be trained here by the best And now your new Masters will make their choices."   3059-8

GARDEN OF DELIGHT   *Sydney St. James*
A vivid account of sexual awakening that follows an innocent but insatiably curious young woman's journey from the furtive, forbidden joys of dormitory life to the unabashed carnality of the wild world. Pretty Pauline blossoms with each new experiment in the sensual arts.   3058-X

STASI SLUT   *Anthony Bobarzynski*
Adina lives in East Germany, far from the sexually liberated, uninhibited debauchery of the West. She meets a group of ruthless and corrupt STASI agents who use her as a pawn in their political chess game as well as for their own gratification until she makes a final bid for total freedom in the revolutionary climax of this *Red*-hot thriller!   3052-0

BLUE TANGO   *Hilary Manning*
Ripe and tempting Julie is haunted by the sounds of extraordinary passion beyond her bedroom wall. Alone at night she fantasizes about taking part in the amorous dramas of her hosts, Claire and Edward. When she finds a way to watch the nightly debauch as well as listen, her insatiable curiosity turns to full-blown lust, her fantasy becomes flesh,and the uncontrollable Julie goes wild with desire!.   3037-7

SEDUCTIONS   *Sincerity Jones*
This original collection includes couplings of every variety, including a woman who helps fulfill her man's fantasy of making it with another man, a dangerous liaison in the back of a taxi, an uncommon alliance between a Wall Street type and a funky downtown woman, and a walk on the wild side for a vacationing sexual adventurer. Thoroughly modern women unleashed in these spicey tales.   83-1

THE CATALYST   *Sara Adamson*
After viewing a controversial, explicitly kinky film full of images of bondage and submission, several audience members find themselves deeply moved by the erotic suggestions they've seen on the screen. Each inspired coupling explorestheir every imagined extreme, as long-denied urges explode with new intensity.   3015-6

LUST   *Palmiro Vicarion*
A wealthy and powerful man of leisure recounts his rise up the corporate ladder and his corresponding descent into debauchery. Adventure and political intrigue provide a stimulating backdrop for this tale of a classic scoundrel with an uncurbed appetite for sexual power!   82-3

WAYWARD   *Peter Jason*
A mysterious countess hires a bus and tour guide for an unusual vacation. Traveling through Europe's most notorious cities and resorts, the bus picks up the countess' friends, lovers, and acquaintances from every walk of life in pursuit of unbridled sensual pleasure. Each guest brings unique sexual tastes and talents to the group, climaxing in countless orgies, outrageous acts, and endless deviation!   3004-0

ASK ISADORA   *Isadora Alman*
Six years of collected columns on sex and relationships. Alman has been called a hip Dr. Ruth and a sexy Dear Abby. Her advice is sharp, funny, and pertinent to anyone experiencing the delights and dilemmas of being a sexual creature in today's perplexing world.   61-0

LOUISE BELHAVEL

FRAGRANT ABUSES

The sex saga of Clara and Iris continues as the now-experienced girls enjoy themselves with a new circle of worldly friends whose imaginations definitely match their own. Against an exotic array of locations, Clara and Iris sample the unique delights of every country and its culture!　　**88-2**

DEPRAVED ANGELS

The final installment in the incredible adventures of Clara and Iris. Together with their friends, lovers, and worldly acquaintances, Clara and Iris explore the frontiers of depravity at home and abroad.　　**92-0**

TITIAN BERESFORD

CINDERELLA

Titian Beresford triumphs again with castle dungeons and tightly corseted ladies-in-waiting, naughty viscounts and impossibly cruel masturbatrixes—nearly every conceivable method of erotic torture is explored and described in lush, vivid detail.　　**3024-5**

CHINA BLUE

KUNG FU NUNS

"When I could stand the pleasure no longer, she lifted me out of the chair and sat me down on top of the table. She then lifted her skirt. The sight of her perfect legs clad in white stockings and a petite garter belt further mesmerized me. I lean particularly towards white garter belts."　　**3031-8**

SECRETS OF THE CITY

China Blue, the infamous Madame of Saigon, a black belt enchantress in the martial arts of love, is out for revenge. Her search brings her to Manhattan, where she intends to call upon her secret sexual arts to kill her enemies at the height of ecstasy. A sex war!　　**03-3**

HARRIET DAIMLER

DARLING • INNOCENCE

In *Darling,* a virgin is raped by a mugger. Driven by her urge for revenge, she searches New York for him in a furious sexual hunt that leads to rape and murder. In *Innocence,* a young invalid determines to experience sex through her voluptuous nurse. Extraordinary erotic imagination!　　**3047-4**

THE PLEASURE THIEVES

They are the Pleasure Thieves, whose sexually preoccupied targets are set up by luscious Carol Stoddard. She forms an ultra-hot sexual threesome with them, trying every combination from two-on-ones to daisy chains—but always on the sly, because pleasures are even sweeter when they're stolen!　　**036-X**

AKBAR DEL PIOMBO

DUKE COSIMO

A kinky, lighthearted romp of non-stop action is played out against the boudoirs, bathrooms and ballrooms of the European nobility, who seem to do nothing all day except each other.　　**3052-0**

A CRUMBLING FAÇADE

The return of that incorrigible rogue, Henry Pike,who continues his pursuit of sex, fair or otherwise, in the most elegant homes of the most irreproachable and debauched aristocrats. **3043-1**

PAULA

"How bad do you want me?" she asked, her voice husky, breathy. I shrank back, for my desire for her was swelling to unspeakable proportions . "Turn around," she said, and I obeyed, willing to do as she asked. **3036-9**

ROBERT DESMOND

PROFESSIONAL CHARMER

A gigolo lives a parasitical life of luxury by providing his sexual services to the rich and bored. Traveling in the most exclusive circles, this gun-for-hire will gratify the lewdest and most vulgar cravings. Every exploit he performs is described in lurid detail in this story of a prostitute's progress! **3003-2**

THE SWEETEST FRUIT

Connie Lashfield is determined to seduce and destroy pious Father Chadcroft to show her former lover that she no longer requires his sexual services. She corrupts the priest into forsaking all that he holds sacred, destroys his peaceful parish, and slyly manipulates him with her smoldering looks and hypnotic sexual aura. **95-5**

MICHAEL DRAX

SILK AND STEEL

"He stood tall and strong in the inky shadows of her room, and Akemi lifted up on her pallet to see the man better, hardly able to believe her luck. Although the man didn't speak a word, Akemi knew what he was there for. He let his robe fall to the floor. Akemi could offer no resistance as the shadowy figure knelt before her, gazing down upon her. Why would she resist? This was what she wanted all along...." **3032-6**

OBSESSIONS

Gorgeous, haughty Victoria is determined to become a top model, using her special abilities to sexually ensnare the powerful men and women who control the fashion industry: the rich voyeur who enjoys photographing Victoria almost as much as she enjoys teasing him; Paige, who finds herself compelled to witness Victoria's conquests; Pietro and Alex, who take turns and then join in for a sizzling threesome. **3012-1**

LIZBETH DUSSEAU

MEMBER OF THE CLUB

"I wondered what would excite me ... And deep down inside, I had the most submissive thoughts: I imagined myself under the spell of mystery, under the grip of men I hardly knew. If there were a club to join, it could take my deepest dreams and make them real. My only question was how far I'd really go. Did I have the nerve to do the things I imagined? Or was I only kidding myself?" A young woman faces the ultimated temptation. **3079-2**

THE APPLICANT

"Adventuresome young woman who enjoys being submissive sought by married couple in early forties. Expect no limits." Hilary answers an ad, hoping to find someone who can meet her special needs. The beautiful Liza turns out to be a flawless mistress, and together with her husband Oliver, she trains Hilary to be the perfect servant. **3038-5**

JOCELYN JOYCE

CAROUSEL

A young American woman leaves her husband when she discovers he is having an affair with their maid. She then becomes the sexual plaything of various Parisian voluptuaries. Wild sex, low morals, and ultimate decadence in the flamboyant years before the European collapse. **3051-2**

SABINE

One of the most unforgettable seductresses ever. No one can refuse her once she casts her spell. And once ensnared, no lover can do anything less than give up his whole life for her. Great men fall at her feet; but she is haughty, distracted, impervious. A mysterious and erotic force. **3046-6**

THREE WOMEN

Dr. Helen Webber finds that her natural authority excites her high-powered lover, Aaron. His daughter Jan is involved in a scorching affair with a married man whose society wife eases her loneliness by slumming at the local watering hole with the regulars. A torrid, tempestuous triangle! **3025-3**

THE WILD HEART

A luxury hotel is the setting for this artful web of sex, desire, and love. A newlywed wife sees sex as a conjugal duty, while her hungry husband tries to awaken her. A ripe Parisian entertains the wealthy guests for the love of money. Each episode provides a new and delicious variation on the old Inn-and-out! **3007-5**

DEMON HEAT

An ancient vampire stalks the unsuspecting in the form of a beautiful woman. Unlike the legendary Dracula, this fiend doesn't drink blood; she craves a different kind of potion. When her insatiable appetite has drained every last drop of juice from her victims, she leaves them spent and hungering for more—even if it means being sucked to death! **79-3**

HAREM SONG

Young, sensuous Amber flees her cruel uncle and provincial English village in search of a better life, but finds she is no match for the glittering lights and mean streets of London. Soon Amber becomes a classy call girl and is eventually sold into a lusty Sultan's harem—a vocation for which she possesses more than average talent! **73-4**

JADE EAST

Laura, passive and passionate, follows her domineering husband Emilio to Hong Kong. He gives her to Wu Li, a Chinese connoisseur of sexual perversions, who passes her on to Madeleine, a flamboyant lesbian. Madeleine's friends make Laura the centerpiece in Hong Kong's underground orgies—where she watches Emilio recruit another lovely young woman. A journey into sexual slavery! **60-2**

RAWHIDE LUST

Diana Beaumont, the young wife of a U.S. Marshal, is kidnapped as an act of vengeance against her husband. Jack Beaumont sets out on a long journey to get his wife back, but finally catches up with her trail only to learn that she's been sold into white slavery in Mexico. A story of the Old West, when the only law was made by the gun, and a woman's virtue was often worth no more than the price of a few steers! **55-6**

THE JAZZ AGE

This is an erotic novel of life in the Roaring Twenties. A Wall Street attorney becomes suspicious of his mistress while his wife has an interlude with a lesbian lover. *The Jazz Age* is a romp of erotic realism in the heyday of the flapper and the speakeasy. **48-3**

THE MASQUERADE LIBRARY

ORDERING IS EASY!

MC/VISA orders can be placed by calling our toll-free number

PHONE 800-458-9640 / FAX 212 986-7355

or mail the coupon below to:

Masquerade Books 801 Second Avenue New York, New York. 10017

BUY ANY FOUR BOOKS AND CHOOSE ONE ADDITIONAL BOOK AS YOUR FREE GIFT.

QTY.	TITLE CDHS 3086-5	NO.	PRICE
	SUBTOTAL		
	POSTAGE & HANDLING		
	TOTAL		

Add $1.00 Postage and Handling for tthe first book and 50¢ for each additional book. Outside the U.S. add $2.00 for the first book, $1.00 for each additional book. New York state residents add 8-1/4% sales tax.

NAME _____

ADDRESS _____ **APT. #** _____

CITY _____ **STATE** _____ **ZIP** _____

TEL. (_____ **)** _____

PAYMENT: ❏ CHECK   ❏ MONEY ORDER   ❏ VISA   ❏ MC

CARD NO. _____ **EXP. DATE** _____

PLEASE ALLOW 4–6 WEEKS DELIVERY. NO C.O.D. ORDERS. PLEASE MAKE ALL CHECKS PAYABLE TO MASQUERADE BOOKS. PAYABLE IN U.S. CURRENCY ONLY